THE ROSE
CHARLES L. HARNESS

"T-PARADOX MEN" ALDISS ~~SPACE OPERA~~ . . . 248
"TIME TRAP" KNIGHT FIRST VOYAGES . . . 213
"AN ORNAMENT TO HIS PROFESSION" MERRIL SF 12 . . . 213
"T-NEW REALITY" SILVERBERG ALPHA 8 . . . 198

A BERKLEY MEDALLION BOOK
PUBLISHED BY
BERKLEY PUBLISHING CORPORATION

Copyright 1953 by Charles L. Harness

All rights reserved

Published by arrangement with the author's agent

BERKLEY MEDALLION EDITION, JANUARY, 1969

---

*BERKLEY MEDALLION BOOKS are published by
Berkley Publishing Corporation
200 Madison Avenue
New York, N.Y. 10016*

BERKLEY MEDALLION BOOKS ® TM 757,375

Printed in the United States of America

INTRODUCTION

by Michael Moorcock

ACCORDING to a close friend of H. J. Campbell, editor of "Authentic SF," the publication of *The Rose* in 1953 marked for Mr. Campbell the zenith of his magazine's career. For him it was never the same again. His feelings were echoed by a multitude of "Authentic" readers, whose letters appeared in succeeding issues.

The Rose was probably one of the most enthusiastically received novels in the history of modern science fiction; old copies of the magazine are still hunted by collectors or treasured by those who bought it at the time; large sums have been offered for copies. In the United States the most stringent and literate critics of SF—people like Judith Merril and Damon Knight—have praised Harness highly, as have Arthur C. Clarke and Brian Aldiss (among others) in this country. Yet the irony is that *The Rose*, Harness's greatest novel, has remained unpublished in book form for over twelve years.

Several factors have contributed to this situation, not least the fact that *The Rose* was published in England at a time when anything called science fiction was frowned upon by the majority of reputable publishers and, appearing as it did in a comparatively obscure British magazine, it never came to the attention of American publishing houses. Also, it was at about this time that Charles Harness stopped writing (he has recently started again after a ten year "rest") and the novel was simply not submitted for book publication.

When, however, the present publisher was shown a tattered copy of "Authentic" containing the novel, he was as enthusiastic about it as I was, and now at last the story can be made available to a wide readership.

Although most of Harness's work is written in the magazine style of the time and at first glance appears to have only the appeal of colorful escapism, reminiscent of A. E. van Vogt or James Blish of the same period, it contains nuances and "throw away" ideas that show a serious (never earnest) mind operating at a much deeper and broader level than its contemporaries. Again, although much of the writing borders on dreamlike surrealism, and some of the incidents have only the scantiest, and barely credible explanations, the plot is fast-moving, never confusing and thoroughly readable.

Yet behind all the extravagance, and making full use of it, is Harness's mind, reasoning (where normally the SF writer rationalizes or reacts) and concerned (where most SF rejects) with the fundamental issues of human existence. If that sounds pompous, rest assured that *The Rose* is never pompous, never pretentious—and this, too, gives it an edge over a lot of better-known SF novels. Like Asimov, who is his only real rival amongst his contemporaries, Harness has an abiding faith in mankind's ability to get itself out of trouble by virtue of its ability to reason.

Much of Harness's work deals with the idea of the superman or, more accurately, the idea of humanity evolving into a "super-human" state. As in *The Rose* and *The New Reality*, there are metaphysical overtones running through virtually everything he has written. Normally I would quarrel with the basic assumptions of such stories, yet I am convinced here that Harness—perhaps not altogether consciously—has made use of fairly conventional SF plot devices of his day in order to symbolize best the basic themes of his work; themes concerned with mankind as it is, rather than mankind as it should be, or even could be.

The theme of *The Rose* asks the old question: "Can science and art be made compatible and complementary?" Harness seems to think they can, and comes up with some spectacular notions of how they can be combined.

The Rose and *The New Reality* (as well as the lighter, less ambitious, *The Chessplayers*) are crammed with delightful notions—what some SF readers call "ideas" —but these are essentially icing on the cake of Harness's fiction. The stories are what too little science fiction is—true stories of ideas, coming to grips with the big abstract problems of human existence and attempting to throw fresh, philosophical light on them. The danger is that the brilliance of fanciful invention in Harness's work might obscure the true themes of the stories and cause them to be dismissed as nothing more than entertaining extravaganzas.

They are, indeed, marvellously entertaining extravaganzas, but I feel that the reader who expects something more than that will find it in this book, for, although Harness has only so much to say about human character, he has a lot to say about the human condition.

MICHAEL MOORCOCK
October 1965

THE ROSE

CHAPTER ONE

HER ballet slippers made a soft slapping sound, moody, mournful, as Anna van Tuyl stepped into the annex of her psychiatrical consulting room and walked toward the tall mirror.

Within seconds she would know whether she was ugly.

As she had done half a thousand times in the past two years, the young woman faced the great glass squarely, brought her arms up gracefully and rose upon her tip-toes. And there resemblance to past hours ceased. She did not proceed to an uneasy study of her face and figure. She could not. For her eyes, as though acting with a wisdom and volition of their own, had closed tightly.

Anna van Tuyl was too much the professional psychiatrist not to recognize that her subconscious mind had shrieked its warning. Eyes still shut, and breathing in great gasps, she dropped from her toes as if to turn and leap away. Then gradually she straightened. She must force herself to go through with it. She might not be able to bring herself here, in this mood of candid receptiveness, twice in one lifetime. It must be now.

She trembled in brief, silent premonition, then quietly raised her eyelids.

Sombre eyes looked out at her, a little darker than yesterday: pools ploughed around by furrows that today gouged a little deeper—the result of months of squinting up from the position into which her spinal deformity had thrust her neck and shoulders. The pale lips were pressed together just a little tighter in their defence against unpredictable pain. The cheeks seemed bloodless having been bleached finally and completely by the Unfinished Dream that haunted her sleep, wherein a nightingale fluttered about a white rose.

As if in brooding confirmation, she brought up simultaneously the pearl-translucent fingers of both hands to the upper borders of her forehead, and there pushed back the incongruous masses of newly-grey hair from two tumorous bulges—like incipient horns. As she did this she made a quarter turn, exposing to the mirror the humped grotesquerie of her back.

Then by degrees, like some netherworld Narcissus, she began to sink under the bizarre enchantment of that misshapen image. She could retain no real awareness that this creature was she. That profile, as if seen through witch-opened eyes, might have been that of some enormous toad, and this flickering metaphor paralyzed her first and only forlorn attempt at identification.

In a vague way, she realized that she had discovered what she had set out to discover. She was ugly. She was even very ugly.

The change must have been gradual, too slow to say of any one day: Yesterday I was not ugly. But even eyes that hungered for deception could no longer deny the cumulative evidence.

So slow—and yet so fast. It seemed only yesterday that had found her face down on Matthew Bell's examination table, biting savagely at a little pillow as his gnarled fingertips probed grimly at her upper thoracic vertebrae.

Well, then, she was ugly. But she'd not give in to self-pity. To hell with what she looked like! To hell with mirrors!

On sudden impulse she seized her balancing tripod with both hands, closed her eyes, and swung.

The tinkling of falling mirror glass had hardly ceased

when a harsh and gravelly voice hailed her from her office. "Bravo!"

She dropped the practice tripod and whirled, aghast. "Matt!"

"Just thought it was time to come in. But if you want to bawl a little, I'll go back out and wait. No?" Without looking directly at her face or pausing for a reply, he tossed a packet on the table. "There it is. Honey, if I could write a ballet score like your *Nightingale and the Rose,* I wouldn't care if my spine was knotted in a figure eight."

"You're crazy," she muttered stonily, unwilling to admit that she was both pleased and curious. "You don't know what it means to have once been able to pirouette, to balance *en arabesque.* And anyway"—she looked at him from the corner of her eye—"how could anyone tell whether the score's good? There's no Finale as yet. It isn't finished."

"Neither is the Mona Lisa, *Kublai Khan,* or a certain symphony by Schubert."

"But this is different. A plotted ballet requires an integrated sequence of events leading up to a climax—to a Finale. I haven't figured out the ending. Did you notice I left a thirty-eight-beat hiatus just before the Nightingale dies? I still need a death song for her. She's entitled to die with a flourish." She couldn't tell him about The Dream—that she always awoke just before that death song began.

"No matter. You'll get it eventually. The story's straight out of Oscar Wilde, isn't it? As I recall, the student needs a red rose as admission to the dance, but his garden contains only white roses. A foolish, if sympathetic nightingale thrusts her heart against a thorn on a white rose stem, and the resultant ill-advised transfusion produces a red rose . . . and a dead nightingale. Isn't that about all there is to it?"

"Almost. But I still need the nightingale's death song. That's the whole point of the ballet. In a plotted ballet, every chord has to be fitted to the immediate action, blended with it, so that it supplements it, explains it, unifies it, and carries the action toward the climax. That death song will make the difference between a good score and a superior one. Don't smile. I think some of my individual scores are rather good, though of course I've never heard them except on my own piano. But without a proper climax, they'll remain unintegrated. They're all variants of some elusive dominating leitmotiv—some really marvellous theme I haven't the greatness of soul to grasp. I know it's something profound and poignant, like the *liebestod* theme in *Tristan*. It probably states a fundamental musical truth, but I don't think I'll ever find it. The nightingale dies with her secret."

She paused, opened her lips as though to continue, and then fell moodily silent again. She wanted to go on talking, to lose herself in volubility. But now the reaction of her struggle with the mirror was setting in, and she was suddenly very tired. Had she ever wanted to cry? Now she thought only of sleep. But a furtive glance at her wristwatch told her it was barely ten o'clock.

The man's craggy eyebrows dropped in an imperceptible frown, faint, yet craftily alert. "Anna, the man who read your *Rose* score wants to talk to you about staging it for the Rose Festival—you know, the annual affair in the Via Rosa."

"I—an unknown—write a Festival ballet?" She added with dry incredulity: "The Ballet Committee is in complete agreement with your friend, of course?"

"He *is* the Committee."

"What did you say his name was?"

"I didn't."

She peered up at him suspiciously. "I can play games, too. If he's so anxious to use my music, why doesn't *he* come to see *me*?"

"He isn't that anxious."

"Oh, a big shot, eh?"

"Not exactly. It's just that he's fundamentally indifferent toward the things that fundamentally interest him. Anyway, he's got a complex about the Via Rosa—loves the district and hates to leave it, even for a few hours."

She rubbed her chin thoughtfully. "Will you believe it, I've never been there. That's the rose-walled district where the ars-gratia-artis professionals live, isn't it? Sort of a plutocratic Rive Gauche?"

The man exhaled in expansive affection. "That's the Via, all right. A six-hundred pound chunk of Carrara marble in every garret, resting most likely on the grand piano.

Poppa chips furiously away with an occasional glance at his model, who is momma, posed *au naturel*."

Anna watched his eyes grow dreamy as he continued. "Momma is a little restless, having suddenly recalled that the baby's bottle and that can of caviar should have come out of the atomic warmer at some nebulous period in the past. Daughter sits before the piano keyboard, surreptitiously switching from Czerny to a torrid little number she's going to try on the trap-drummer in Dorran's Via orchestra. Beneath the piano are the baby and mongrel pup. Despite their tender age, this thing is already in their blood. Or at least, their stomachs, for they have just finished an *hors d'oeuvre* of marble chips and now amiably share the *pièce de résistance*, a battered but rewarding tube of Van Dyke brown."

Anna listened to this with widening eyes. Finally she gave a short amazed laugh. "Matt Bell, you really love that life, don't you?"

He smiled. "In some ways the creative life is pretty carefree. I'm just a psychiatrist specializing in psychogenetics. I don't know an arpeggio from a drypoint etching, but I like to be around people that do." He bent forward earnestly. "These artists—these golden people—they're the coming force in society. And you're one of them, Anna, whether you know it or like it. You and your kind are going to inherit the earth—only you'd better hurry if you don't want Martha Jacques and her National Security scientists to get it first. So the battle lines converge in Renaissance II. Art versus Science. Who dies? Who lives?" He looked thoughtful, lonely. He might have been pursuing an introspective monologue in the solitude of his own chambers.

"This Mrs. Jacques," said Anna. "What's she like? You asked me to see her tomorrow about her husband, you know."

"Darn good looking woman. The most valuable mind in history, some say. And if she really works out something concrete from her Sciomnia equation, I guess there won't be any doubt about it. And that's what makes her potentially the most dangerous human being alive: National Security is fully aware of her value, and they'll coddle her tiniest whim—at least until she pulls something tangible out of Sciomnia. Her main whim for the past few years has been her errant husband, Mr. Ruy Jacques."

"Do you think she really loves him?"

"Just between me and you she hates his guts. So naturally she doesn't want any other woman to get him. She has him watched, of course. The Security Bureau co-operate with alacrity, because they don't want foreign agents to approach *her* through *him*. There have been ugly rumors of assassinated models . . . But I'm digressing." He cocked a quizzical eye at her. "Permit me to repeat the invitation of your unknown admirer. Like you, he's another true child of the new Renaissance. The two of you should find much in common—more than you can now guess. I'm very serious about this, Anna. Seek him out immediately—tonight—now. There aren't any mirrors in the Via."

"Please, Matt."

"Honey," he growled, "to a man my age you aren't ugly. And this man's the same. If a woman is pretty, he paints her and forgets her. But if she's some kind of an artist, he talks to her, and he can get rather endless sometimes. If it's any help to your self-assurance, he's about the homeliest creature on the face of the earth. You'll look like De Milo alongside him."

The woman laughed shortly. "I can't get mad at you, can I? Is he married?"

"Sort of." His eyes twinkled. "But don't let that concern you. He's a perfect scoundrel."

"Suppose I decide to look him up. Do I simply run up and down the Via paging all homely friends of Dr. Matthew Bell?"

"Not quite. If I were you I'd start at the entrance—where they have all those queer side-shows and one-man exhibitions. Go on past the vendress of love philters and work down the street until you find a man in a white suit with polka dots."

"How perfectly odd! And then what? How can I introduce myself to a man whose name I don't know? Oh, Matt, this is so silly, so *childish* . . ."

He shook his head in slow denial. "You aren't going to think about names when you see him. And your name won't mean a thing to him, anyway. You'll be lucky if you aren't 'hey you' by midnight. But it isn't going to matter."

"It isn't too clear why you don't offer to escort me."

10

She studied him calculatingly. "And I think you're withholding his name because you know I wouldn't go if you revealed it."

He merely chuckled.

She lashed out: "Damn you, get me a cab."

"I've had one waiting half an hour."

CHAPTER TWO

"TELL ya what the professor's gonna do, ladies and gentlemen. He's gonna defend not just one paradox. Not just two. Not just a dozen. No, ladies and gentlemen, the professor's gonna defend *seventeen,* and all in the space of one short hour, without repeating himself, and including a brand-new one he has just thought up today: 'Music owes its meaning to its ambiguity.' Remember, folks, an axiom is just a paradox the professor's already got hold of. The cost of this dazzling display . . . don't crowd there, mister . . ."

Anna felt a relaxing warmth flowing over her mind, washing at the encrusted strain of the past hour. She smiled and elbowed her way through the throng and on down the street, where a garishly lighted sign, bat-wing doors, and a forlorn cluster of waiting women announced the next attraction:

"FOR MEN ONLY. Daring blindfold exhibitions and variety entertainments continuously."

Inside, a loudspeaker was blaring: "Thus we have seen how to compose the ideal end-game problem in chess. And now, gentlemen, for the small consideration of an additional quarter . . ."

But Anna's attention was now occupied by a harsh cawing from across the street.

"Love philters! Works on male or female! Any age! Never fails!"

She laughed aloud. Good old Matt! He had foreseen

what these glaring multifaceted nonsensical stimuli would do for her. Love philters! Just what she needed!

The vendress of love philters was of ancent vintage, perhaps seventy-five years old. Above cheeks of wrinkled leather her eyes glittered speculatively. And how weirdly she was clothed! Her bedraggled dress was a shrieking purple. And under that dress was another of the same hue, though perhaps a little faded. And under *that,* still another.

"That's why they call me Violet," cackled the old woman, catching Anna's stare. "Better come over and let me mix you one."

But Anna shook her head and passed on, eyes shining. Fifteen minutes later, as she neared the central Via area, her receptive reverie was interrupted by the outburst of music ahead.

Good! Watching the street dancers for half an hour would provide a highly pleasant climax to her escapade. Apparently there wasn't going to be any man in a polka dot suit. Matt was going to be disappointed but it certainly wasn't her fault she hadn't found him.

There was something oddly familiar about that music.

She quickened her pace, and then, as recognition came, she began to run as fast as her crouching back would permit. This was *her* music—the prelude to Act III of her ballet!

She burst through the mass of spectators lining the dance square. The music stopped. She stared out into the scattered dancers, and what she saw staggered the twisted frame of her slight body. She fought to get air through her vacuously-wide mouth.

In one unearthly instant, a rift had threaded its way through the dancer-packed square, and a pasty white face, altogether spectral, had looked down that open rift into hers. A face over a body that was enveloped in a strange glowing gown of shimmering white. She thought he had also been wearing a white academic mortar board, but the swarming dancers closed in again before she could be sure.

She fought an unreasoning impulse to run.

Then, as quickly as it had come, logic reasserted itself; the shock was over. Odd costumes were no rarity on the Via. There was no cause for alarm.

She was breathing almost normally when the music died away and someone began a harsh harangue over the public address system. "Ladies and gentlemen, it is our rare good fortune to have with us tonight the genius who composed the music you have been enjoying."

A sudden burst of laughter greeted this, seeming to originate in the direction of the orchestra, and was counterpointed by an uncomplimentary blare from one of the horns.

"Your mockery is misplaced, my friends. It just so happens that this genius is not I, but another. And since she has thus far had no opportunity to join in the revelry, your inimitable friend, as The Student, will take her hand, as The Nightingale, in the final *pas de deux* from Act III. That should delight her, yes?"

The address system clicked off amid clapping and a buzz of excited voices, punctuated by occasional shouts.

She must escape! She must get away!

Anna pressed back into the crowd. There was no longer any question about finding a man in a polka dot suit. *That* creature in white certainly wasn't he. Though how could he have recognized her?

She hesitated. Perhaps he had a message from the other one, if there really was one with polka dots.

No, she'd better go. This was turning out to be more of a nightmare than a lark.

Still——

She peeked back from behind the safety of a woman's sleeve, and after a moment located the man in white.

His pasty-white face with its searching eyes was much closer. But what had happened to his *white* cap and gown? *Now*, they weren't white at all! What optical fantasy was this? She rubbed her eyes and looked again.

The cap and gown seemed to be made up of green and purple polka dots on a white background! So he was her man!

She could see him now as the couples spread out before him, exchanging words she couldn't hear, but which seemed to carry an irresistible laugh response.

Very well, she'd wait.

Now that everything was cleared up and she was safe again behind her armor of objectivity, she studied him with growing curiosity. Since that first time she had never again got a good look at him. Someone always seemed to get in the way. It was almost, she thought, as though he was working his way out toward her, taking every advantage of human cover, like a hunter closing in on wary quarry, until it was too late . . .

He stood before her.

There were harsh clanging sounds as his eyes locked with hers. Under that feral scrutiny the woman maintained her mental balance by the narrowest margin.

The Student.

The Nightingale, for love of The Student, makes a Red Rose. An odious liquid was burning in her throat, but she couldn't swallow.

Gradually she forced herself into awareness of a twisted, sardonic mouth framed between aquiline nose and jutting chin. The face, plastered as it was by white powder, had revealed no distinguishing features beyond its unusual size. Much of the brow was obscured by the many tassels dangling over the front of his travestied mortarboard cap. Perhaps the most striking thing about the man was not his face, but his body. It was evident that he had some physical deformity, to outward appearances not unlike her own. She knew intuitively that he was not a true hunchback. His chest and shoulders were excessively broad, and he seemed, like her, to carry a mass of superfluous tissue on his upper thoracic vertebrae. She surmised that the scapulae would be completely obscured.

His mouth twisted in subtle mockery. "Bell said you'd come." He bowed and held out his right hand.

"It is very difficult for me to dance," she pleaded in a low hurried voice. "I'd humiliate us both.'

"I'm no better at this than you, and probably worse. But I'd never give up dancing merely because someone might think I look awkward. Come, we'll use the simplest steps."

There was something harsh and resonant in his voice that reminded her of Matt Bell. Only . . . Bell's voice had never set her stomach churning.

He held out his other hand.

Behind him the dancers had retreated to the edge of the square, leaving the centre empty, and the first beats of her music from the orchestra pavilion floated to her with ecstatic clarity.

Just the two of them, out there . . . before a thousand eyes. . . .

Subconsciously she followed the music. There was her cue—the signal for the Nightingale to fly to her fatal assignation with the white rose.

She must reach out both perspiring hands to this stranger, must blend her deformed body into his equally misshapen one. She must, because he was The Student, and she was The Nightingale.

She moved toward him silently and took his hands.

As she danced, the harsh-lit street and faces seemed gradually to vanish. Even The Student faded into the barely perceptible distance, and she gave herself up to The Unfinished Dream.

CHAPTER THREE

SHE dreamed that she danced alone in the moonlight, that she fluttered in solitary circles in the moonlight, fastened and appalled by the thing she must do to create a Red Rose. She dreamed that she sang a strange and magic song, a wondrous series of chords, the song she had so long sought. Pain buoyed her on excruciating wings, then flung her heavily to earth. The Red Rose was made, and she was dead.

She groaned and struggled to sit up.

Eyes glinted at her out of pasty whiteness. "That was quite a *pas*—only more *de seul* than *de deux*," said the Student.

She looked about in uneasy wonder.

They were sitting together on a marble bench before a fountain. Behind them was a curved walk bounded by a high wall covered with climbing green, dotted here and there with white.

She put her hand to her forehead. "Where are we?"

"This is White Rose Park."

"How did I get here?"

"You danced in on your own two feet through the archway yonder."

"I don't remember . . ."

"I thought perhaps you were trying to lend a bit of realism to the part. But you're early."

"What do you mean?"

"There are only white roses growing in here, and even *they* won't be in full bloom for another month. In late June they'll be a real spectacle. You mean you didn't know about this little park?"

"No. I've never ever been in the Via before. And yet . . ."

"And yet what?"

She hadn't been able to tell anyone—not even Matt Bell—what she was now going to tell this man, an utter stranger, her companion of an hour. He had to be told because, somehow, he too was caught up in the dream ballet.

She began haltingly. "Perhaps I *do* know about this place. Perhaps someone told me about it, and the information got buried in my subconscious mind until I wanted a white rose. There's really something behind my ballet that Dr. Bell didn't tell you. He couldn't, because I'm the only one who knows. The *Rose* comes from my dreams. Only, a better word is nightmares. Every night the score starts from the beginning. In the dream, I dance. Every night, for months and months, there was a little more music, a little more dancing. I tried to get it out of my head, but I couldn't. I started writing it down, the music and the choreography."

The man's unsmiling eyes were fixed on her face in deep absorption.

Thus encouraged, she continued. "For the past several nights I have dreamed almost the complete ballet, right up to the death of the nightingale. I suppose I identify myself so completely with the nightingale that I subconsciously censor her song as she presses her breast against the thorn on the white rose. That's where I always awakened, or at least, always did before tonight. But I think I heard the music tonight. It's a series of chords . . . thirty-eight chords, I believe. The first nineteen were frightful, but the second nineteen were marvellous. Everything was too real to wake up. The Student, The Nightingale, The White Roses."

But now the man threw back his head and laughed raucously. "You ought to see a psychiatrist!"

Anna bowed her head humbly.

"Oh, don't take it too hard," he said. "My wife's even after *me* to see a psychiatrist."

"Really?" Anna was suddenly alert. "What seems to be wrong with you? I mean, what does she object to?"

"In general, my laziness. In particular, it seems I've forgotten how to read and write." He gave her widening eyes a sidelong look. "I'm a perfect parasite, too. Haven't done any real work in months. What would *you* call it if you couldn't work until you had the final measures of the *Rose,* and you kept waiting, and nothing happened?"

"Hell."

He was glumly silent.

Anna asked, hesitantly, yet with a growing certainty. "This thing you're waiting for . . . might it have anything to do with the ballet? Or to phrase it from your point of view, do you think the completion of my ballet may help answer your problem?"

"Might. Couldn't say."

She continued quietly. "You're going to have to face it eventually, you know. Your psychiatrist is going to ask you. How will you answer?"

"I won't. I'll tell him to go to the devil."

"How can you be so sure he's a *he*?"

"Oh? Well, if he's a *she,* she might be willing to pose *al fresco* an hour or so. The model shortage is quite grave you know, with all of the little dears trying to be painters."

"But if she doesn't have a good figure?"

"Well, maybe her face has some interesting possibilities. It's a rare woman who's a total physical loss."

Anna's voice was very low. "But what if *all* of her were very ugly? What if your proposed psychiatrist were me, *Mr. Ruy Jacques*?"

His great dark eyes blinked, then his lips pursed and exploded into insane laughter. He stood up suddenly. "Come, my dear, whatever your name is, and let the blind lead the blind."

"Anna van Tuyl," she told him, smiling.

She took his arm. Together they strolled around the arc of the walk toward the entrance arch.

She was filled with a strange contentment.

Over the green-crested wall at her left, day was about to break, and from the Via came the sound of groups of diehard revellers, breaking up and drifting away, like spectres at cock-crow. The cheerful clatter of milk bottles got mixed up in it somehow.

They paused at the archway while the man kicked at the seat of the pants of a spectre whom dawn had returned to slumber beneath the arch. The sleeper cursed and stumbled to his feet in bleary indignation.

"Excuse us, Willie," said Anna's companion, motioning for her to step through.

She did, and the creature of the night at once dropped into his former sprawl.

Anna cleared her throat. "Where now?"

"At this point I must cease to be a gentleman, *I'm* returning to the studio for some sleep, and *you* can't come. For, if your physical energy is inexhaustible, mine is not." He raised a hand as her startled mouth dropped open. "Please, dear Anna, don't insist. Some other night, perhaps."

"Why, you——"

"Tut tut." He turned a little and kicked again at the sleeping man. "I'm not an utter cad, you know. I would never abandon a weak, frail, unprotected woman in the Via."

She was too amazed now even to splutter.

Ruy Jacques reached down and pulled the drunk up against the wall of the arch, where he held him firmly. "Dr. Anna van Tuyl, may I present Willie the Cork."

The Cork grinned at her in unfocused somnolence.

"Most people call him the Cork because, that's what seals in the bottle's contents," said Jacques. "*I* call him the Cork because he's always bobbing up. He looks like a bum, but that's just because he's a good actor. He's really a Security man tailing me at my wife's request, and he'd only be too delighted for a little further conversation with you. A cheery good morning to you both!"

A milk truck wheeled around the corner. Jacques leaped for its running board, and he was gone before the psychiatrist could voice the protest boiling up in her.

A gurgling sigh at her feet drew her eyes down momentarily. The Cork was apparently bobbing once more on his own private alcoholic ocean.

Anna snorted in mingled disgust and amusement, then hailed a cab. As she slammed the door, she took one last look at Willie. Not until the cab rounded the corner and cut off his muffled snores did she realize that people usually don't snore with their eyes half-opened and looking at you, especially with eyes no longer blurred with sleep, but hard and glinting.

CHAPTER FOUR

TWELVE hours later, in another cab and in a different part of the city, Anna peered absently out at the stream of traffic. Her mind was on the coming conference with Martha Jacques. Only twelve hours ago Mrs. Jacques had been just a bit of necessary case history. Twelve hours ago Anna hadn't really cared whether Mrs. Jacques followed Bell's recommendation and gave her the case. Now it was all different. She wanted the case, and she was going to get it.

Ruy Jacques—how many hours awaited her with this amazing scoundrel, this virtuoso of liberal—nay, loose—arts, who held locked within his remarkable mind the missing pieces of their joint jigsaw puzzle of The Rose?

That jeering, mocking face—what would it look like without makeup? Very ugly, she hoped. Beside his, her own face wasn't too bad.

Only—he was married, and she was en route at this moment to discuss preliminary matters with his wife, who, even if she no longer loved him, at least had prior rights to him. There were considerations of professional ethics even in thinking about him. Not that she could ever fall in love with him or any other patient. Particularly with one who had treated her so cavalierly. Willie the Cork, indeed!

As she waited in the cold silence of the great antechamber adjoining the office of Martha Jacques, Anna sensed that she was being watched. She was quite certain that by now she'd been photographed, x-rayed for hidden weapons, and her fingerprints taken from her professional card. In colossal central police files a thousand miles away, a bored clerk would be leafing through her dossier for the benefit of Colonel Grade's visigraph in the office beyond.

In a moment——

"Dr. van Tuyl to see Mrs. Jacques. Please enter door B-3," said the tinny voice of the intercom.

She followed a guard to the door, which he opened for her.

This room was smaller. At the far end a woman, a very lovely woman, whom she took to be Martha Jacques, sat peering in deep abstraction at something on the desk before her. Beside the desk, and slightly to the rear, a moustached man in plain clothes stood, reconnoitring Anna with hawklike eyes. The description fitted what Anna had heard of Colonel Grade, Chief of the National Security Bureau.

Grade stepped forward and introduced himself curtly, then presented Anna to Mrs. Jacques.

And then the psychiatrist found her eyes fastened to a sheet of paper on Mrs. Jacques' desk. And as she stared, she felt a sharp dagger of ice sinking into her spine, and she grew slowly aware of a background of brooding whispers in her mind, heart-constricting in their suggestions of mental disintegration.

For the thing drawn on the paper, in red ink, was—although warped, incomplete, and misshapen—unmistakably a rose.

"Mrs. Jacques!" cried Grade.

Martha Jacques must have divined simultaneously Anna's great interest in the paper. With an apologetic murmur she turned it face down. "Security regulations, you know. I'm really supposed to keep it locked up in the presence of visitors." Even a murmur could not hide the harsh metallic quality of her voice.

So *that* was why the famous Sciomnia formula was sometimes called the "Jacques Rosette": when traced in an everexpanding wavering red spiral in polar coordinates, it was . . . a Red Rose.

The explanation brought at once a feeling of relief and a sinister deepening of the sense of doom that had overshadowed her for months. So you, too, she thought wonderingly, seek The Rose. Your artist-husband is wretched for want of it, and now you. But do you seek the same rose? Is the rose of the scientist the true rose, and Ruy Jacques' the false? What *is* the rose? Will I ever know?

Grade broke in. "Your brilliant reputation is deceptive, Dr. van Tuyl. From Dr. Bell's description, we had pictured you as an older woman."

"Yes," said Martha Jacques, studying her curiously. "We really had in mind an older woman, one less likely to . . . to——"

"To involve your husband emotionally?"

"Exactly," said Grade. "Mrs. Jacques must have her mind completely free from distractions. However"—he turned to the woman scientist—"it is my studied opinion that we need not anticipate difficulty from Dr. van Tuyl on that account."

Anna felt her throat and cheeks going hot as Mrs. Jacques nodded in damning agreement: "I think you're right, Colonel."

"Of course," said Grade, "*Mr.* Jacques may not accept her."

"That remains to be seen," said Martha Jacques. "He might tolerate a fellow artist." To Anna: "Dr. Bell tells us that you compose music, or something like that?"

"Something like that," nodded Anna. She wasn't worried. It was a question of waiting. This woman's murderous jealousy, though it might some day destroy her, at the moment concerned her not a whit.

Colonel Grade said: "Mrs. Jacques has probably warned you that her husband is somewhat eccentric; he may be somewhat difficult to deal with at times. On this account, the Security Bureau is prepared to triple your fee, if we find you acceptable."

Anna nodded gravely. Ruy Jacques and money, too!

"For most of your consultations you'll have to track him down," said Martha Jacques. "He'll never come to you. But considering what we're prepared to pay, this inconvenience should be immaterial."

Anna thought briefly of that fantastic creature who had singled her out of a thousand faces. "That will be satisfactory. And now, Mrs. Jacques, for my preliminary orientation, suppose you describe some of the more striking behaviorisms that you've noted in your husband."

"Certainly. Dr. Bell, I presume, has already told you that Ruy has lost the ability to read and write. Ordinarily that's indicative of advanced dementia praecox, isn't it? However, I think Mr. Jacques' case presents a more complicated picture, and my own guess is schizophrenia rather than dementia. The dominant and most frequently observed psyche is a megalomanic phase, during which he tends to harangue his listeners on various odd subjects. We've picked up some of these speeches on a hidden recorder and made a Zipf analysis of the word-frequencies."

Anna's brows creased dubiously. "A Zipf count is pretty mechanical."

"But scientific, undeniably scientific. I have made a careful study of the method, and can speak authoritatively. Back in the forties Zipf of Harvard proved that in a representative sample of English, the interval separating the repetition of the same word was inversely proportional to its frequency. He provided a mathematical formula for something previously known only qualitatively: that a too-soon repetition of the same or similar sound is distracting and grating to the cultured mind. If we must say the same thing in the next paragraph, we avoid repetition with an appropriate synonym. But not the schizophrenic. His disease disrupts his higher centres of association, and certain discriminating neural networks are no longer available for his writing and speech. He has no compunction against immediate and continuous tonal repetition."

"A rose is a rose is a rose . . ." murmured Anna.

"Eh? How did you know what this transcription was about? Oh, you were just quoting Gertrude Stein? Well, I've read about her, and she proves my point. She admitted that she wrote under autohypnosis, which we'd call a light case of schizo. But she could be normal, too. My husband never is. He goes on like this all the time. This was transcribed from one of his monologues. Just listen:

" 'Behold, Willie, through yonder window the symbol of your mistress' defeat: The Rose! The rose, my dear Willie, grows not in murky air. The smoky metropolis of yester-year drove it to the country. But now, with the unsullied skyline of your atomic age, the red rose returns. How mysterious, Willie, that the rose continues to offer herself to us dull, plodding humans. We see nothing in her but a pretty flower. Her regretful thorns forever declare our inept clumsiness, and her lack of honey chides our gross sensuality. Ah, Willie, let us become as birds! For only the winged can eat the fruit of the rose and spread her pollen . . .' "

Mrs. Jacques looked up at Anna. "Did you keep count? He used the word 'rose' no less than five times, when once or twice was sufficient. He certainly had no lack of mellifluous synonyms at his disposal, such as 'red flower,' 'thorned plant,' and so on. And instead of saying 'the red rose returns' he should have said something like 'it comes back'."

"And lose the triple alliteration?" smiled Anna. "No, Mrs. Jacques, I'd re-examine that diagnosis very critically. Everyone who talks like a poet isn't necessarily insane."

A tiny bell began to jangle on a massive metal door in the right-hand wall.

"A message for me," growled Grade. "Let it wait."

"We don't mind," said Anna, "if you want to have it sent in."

"It isn't *that*. That's my private door, and I'm the only one who knows the combination. But I told them not to interrupt us, unless it dealt with this specific interview."

Anna thought of the eyes of Willie the Cork, hard and glistening. Suddenly she knew that Ruy Jacques had not been joking about the identity of the man. Was The Cork's report just now getting on her dossier? Mrs. Jacques wasn't going to like it. Suppose they turned her down. Would she dare seek out Ruy Jacques under the noses of Grade's trigger men?

"Damn that fool," muttered Grade. "I left strict orders about being disturbed. Excuse me."

He strode angrily toward the door. After a few seconds of dial manipulation, he turned the handle and pulled it inward. A hand thrust something metallic at him. Anna caught whispers. She fought down a feeling of suffocation as Grade opened the cassette and read the message.

The Security officer walked leisurely back toward them. He stroked his moustache coolly, handed the bit of paper to Martha Jacques, then clasped his hands behind his back. For a moment he looked like a glowering bronze statue. "Dr. van Tuyl, you didn't tell us that you were already acquainted with Mr. Jacques. Why?"

"You didn't ask me."

Martha Jacques said harshly: "That answer is hardly satisfactory. How long have you known Mr. Jacques? I want to get to the bottom of this."

"I met him last night for the first time in the Via Rosa. We danced. That's all. The whole thing was purest coincidence."

"You are his lover," accused Martha Jacques.

Anna colored. "You flatter me, Mrs. Jacques."

Grade coughed. "She's right. Mrs. Jacques. I see no sex-based espionage."

"Then maybe it's even subtler," said Martha Jacques. "These platonic females are still worse, because they sail under false colors. She's after Ruy, I tell you."

"I assure you," said Anna, "that your reaction comes as a complete surprise to me. Naturally, I shall withdraw from the case at once."

"But it doesn't end with that," said Grade curtly. "The national safety may depend on Mrs. Jacques' peace of mind during the coming weeks. I *must* ascertain your relation with Mr. Jacques. And I must warn you that if a compromising situation exists, the consequences will be most unpleasant." He picked up the telephone. "Grade. Get me the O.D."

Anna's palms were uncomfortably wet and sticky. She wanted to wipe them on the sides of her dress, but then decided it would be better to conceal all signs of nervousness.

Grade barked into the mouthpiece. "Hello! That you, Packard? Send me——"

Suddenly the room vibrated with the shattering impact of massive metal on metal.

The three whirled toward the sound.

A stooped, loudly dressed figure was walking away from the great and inviolate door of Colonel Grade, drinking in with sardonic amusement the stuporous faces turned to him. It was evident he had just slammed the door behind him with all his strength.

Insistent squeakings from the teleset stirred Grade into a feeble response. "Never mind . . . it's Mr. Jacques . . ."

CHAPTER FIVE

THE swart ugliness of that face verged on the sublime. Anna observed for the first time the two horn-like protuberances on his forehead, which the man made no effort to conceal. His black woollen beret was cocked jauntily over one horn; the other, the visible one, bulged even more than Anna's horns, and to her fascinated eyes he appeared as some Greek satyr; Silenus with an eternal hangover, or Pan wearying of fruitless pursuit of fleeting nymphs. It was the face of a cynical post-gaol Wilde, of a Rimbaud, of a Goya turning his brush in saturnine glee from Spanish grandees to the horror-world of Ensayos.

Like a phantom voice Matthew Bell's cryptic prediction seemed to float into her ears again: ". . . much in common . . . more than you guess . . ."

There was so little time to think. Ruy Jacques must have recognized her frontal deformities even while that tasselated mortar-board of his Student costume had prevented her from seeing his. He must have identified her as a less advanced case of his own disease. Had he foreseen the turn of events here? Was he here to protect the only person on earth who might help him? That wasn't like him. He just wasn't the sensible type. She got the uneasy impression that he was here solely for his own amusement—simply to make fools of the three of them.

Grade began to sputter. "Now see here, Mr. Jacques. It's impossible to get in through that door. It's my private entrance. I changed the combination myself only this morning." The moustache bristled indignantly. "I must ask the meaning of this."

"Pray do, Colonel, pray do."

"Well, then, what is the meaning of this?"

"None, Colonel. Have you no faith in your own syllogisms? No one can open your private door but you. Q.E.D. No one did. I'm not really here. No smiles? Tsk tsk! Paragraph 6, p. 80 of the Manual of Permissible Military Humor officially recognizes the paradox."

"There's no such publication——" stormed Grade.

But Jacques brushed him aside. He seemed now to notice Anna for the first time, and bowed with exaggerated punctilio. "My profound apologies, madame. You were standing so still, so quiet, that I mistook you for a rose bush." He beamed at each in turn. "Now isn't this delightful? I feel like a literary lion. It's the first time in my life that my admirers ever met for the express purpose of discussing my work."

How could he know that we were discussing his "composition," wondered Anna. *And how did he open the door?*

"If you'd eavesdropped long enough," said Martha Jacques, "you'd have learned we weren't admiring your 'prose poem'. In fact, I think it's pure nonsense."

No, thought Anna, he couldn't have eavesdropped, because we didn't talk about his speech after Grade opened the door. There's something here—in this room—that *tells* him.

"You don't even think it's poetry?" repeated Jacques, wide-eyed. "Martha, coming from one with your scientifically developed poetical sense, this is utterly damning."

"There *are* certain well recognized approaches to the appreciation of poetry," said Martha Jacques doggedly. "You ought to have the autoscanner read you some books on the aesthetic laws of language. It's all there."

The artist blinked in great innocence. "*What's* all there?"

"Scientific rules for analyzing poetry. Take the mood of a poem. You can very easily learn whether it's gay or sombre just by comparing the proportion of low-pitched vowels—*u* and *o*, that is—to the high-pitched vowels—*a*, *e* and *i*."

"Well, what do you know about that!" He turned a wondering face to Anna. "And she's right! Come to think of it, in Milton's *L'Allegro*, most of the vowels are high-pitched, while in his *Il Penseroso*, they're mostly low-pitched. Folks, I believe we've finally found a yardstick for genuine poetry. No longer must we flounder in poetastical soup. Now let's see." He rubbed his chin in blank-faced thoughtfulness. "Do you know, for years I've considered Swinburne's lines mourning Charles Baudelaire to be the distillate of sadness. But that, of course, was before I had heard of Martha's scientific approach, and had to rely solely on my unsophisticated, untrained, uninformed feelings. How stupid I was! For the thing is crammed with high-pitched vowels, and long *e* dominates: 'thee,' 'sea,' 'weave,' 'eve,' 'heat,' 'sweet,' 'feet' . . ." He struck his brow as if in sudden comprehension. "Why, it's gay! I must set it to a snappy polka!"

"Drivel," sniffed Martha Jacques. "Science——"

"——is simply a parasitical, adjectival, and useless occupation devoted to the quantitative restatement of Art," finished the smiling Jacques. "Science is functionally sterile; it creates nothing; it says nothing new. The scientist can never be more than a humble camp-follower of the artist. There exists no scientific truism that hasn't been anticipated by creative art. The examples are endless. Uccello worked out mathematically the laws of perspective in the fifteenth century; but Kallicrates applied the same laws two thousand years before in designing the columns of the Parthenon. The Curies thought they invented the idea of 'half-life'—of a thing vanishing in proportion to its residue. The Egyptians tuned their lyre-strings to dampen according to the same formula. Napier thought he invented logarithms—entirely overlooking the fact that the Roman brass workers flared their trumpets to follow a logarithmic curve."

"You're deliberately selecting isolated examples," retorted Martha Jacques.

"Then suppose you name a few so-called scientific discoveries," replied the man. "I'll prove they were scooped by an artist, every time."

"I certainly shall. How about Boyle's gas law? I suppose you'll say Praxiteles knew all along that gas pressure runs inversely proportional to its volume at a given temperature?"

"I expected something more sophisticated. That one's

too easy. Boyle's gas law, Hooke's law of springs, Galileo's law of pendulums, and a host of similar hogwash simply state that compression, kinetic energy, or whatever name you give it, is inversely proportional to its reduced dimensions, and is proportional to the amount of its displacement in the total system. Or, as the artist says, impact results from, and is proportional to, displacement of an object within its milieu. Could the final couplet of a Shakespearean sonnet enthral us if our minds hadn't been conditioned, held in check, and compressed in suspense by the preceding fourteen lines? Note how cleverly Donne's famous poem builds up to its crash line, 'It tolls for thee!' By blood, sweat, and genius, the Elizabethans lowered the entropy of their creations in precisely the same manner and with precisely the same result as when Boyle compressed his gases. And the method was long old when *they* were young. It was old when the Ming artists were painting the barest suggestions of landscapes on the disproportionate backgrounds of their vases. The Shah Jahan was aware of it when he designed the long eye-restraining reflecting pool before the Taj Mahal. The Greek tragedians knew it. Sophocles' *Oedipus* is still unparalleled in its suspensive pacing toward climax. Solomon's imported Chaldean arthitects knew the effect to be gained by spacing the Holy of Holies at a distance from the temple pylae, and the Cro-Magnard magicians with malice aforethought painted their marvellous animal scenes only in the most inaccessible crannies of their limestone caves."

Martha Jacques smiled coldly. "Drivel, drivel, drivel. But never mind. One of these days soon I'll produce evidence you'll be *forced* to admit art can't touch."

"If you're talking about Sciomnia, there's *real* nonsense for you," countered Jacques amiably. "Really, Martha, it's a frightful waste of time to reconcile biological theory with the unified field theory of Einstein, which itself merely reconciles the relativity and quantum theories, a futile gesture in the first place. Before Einstein announced *his* unified theory in 1949, the professors handled the problem very neatly. They taught the quantum theory on Mondays, Wednesdays and Fridays and the relativity theory on Tuesdays, Thursdays and Saturdays. On the Sabbath they rested in front of their television sets. What's the good of Sciomnia, anyway?"

"It's the final summation of all physical and biological knowledge," retorted Martha Jacques. "And as such, Sciomnia represents the highest possible aim of human endeavor. Man's goal in life is to understand his environment, to analyze it to the last iota—to know what he controls. The first person to understand Sciomnia may well rule not only this planet, but the whole galaxy—not that he'd want to, but he could. That person may not be me—but will certainly be a scientist, and not an irresponsible artist."

"But Martha," protested Jacques. "Where did you pick up such a weird philosophy? The highest aim of man is *not* to analyze, but to synthesize—to *create*. If you ever solve all of the nineteen sub-equations of Sciomnia, you'll be at a dead end. There'll be nothing left to analyze. As Dr. Bell the psychogeneticist says, overspecialization, be it mental, as in the human scientist, or dental, as in the sabre-tooth tiger, is just a synonym for extinction. But if we continue to create, we shall eventually discover how to transcend——"

Grade coughed, and Martha Jacques cut in tersely: "Never mind what Dr. Bell says. Ruy, have you ever seen this woman before?"

"The rose bush? Hmm." He stepped over to Anna and looked squarely down at her face. She flushed and looked away. He circled her in slow, critical appraisal, like a prospective buyer in a slave market of ancient Baghdad. "Hmm," he repeated doubtfully.

Anna breathed faster; her cheeks were the hue of beets. But she couldn't work up any sense of indignity. On the contrary, there was something illogically delicious about being visually pawed and handled by this strange leering creature.

Then she jerked visibly. What hypnotic insanity was this? This man held her life in the palm of his hand. If he acknowledged her, the vindictive creature who passed as his wife would crush her professionally. If he denied her, they'd know he was lying to save her—and the consequences might prove even less pleasant. And what difference would her ruin make to *him*? She had sensed at once his monumental selfishness. And even if that conceit, that gorgeous self-love urged him to preserve her for her hypothetical value in finishing up the Rose score, she didn't see how he was going to manage it.

"Do you recognize her, Mr. Jacques," demanded Grade.

"I do," came the solemn reply.

Anna stiffened.

Martha Jacques smiled thinly. "Who is she?"

"Miss Ethel Twinkham, my old spelling teacher. How are you, Miss Twinkham? What brings you out of retirement?"

"I'm not Miss Twinkham," said Anna dryly. "My name is Anna van Tuyl. For your information, we met last night in the Via Rosa."

"Oh! Of course!" He laughed happily. "I seem to remember now, quite indistinctly. And I want to apologize, Miss Twinkham. My behavior was execrable, I suppose. Anyway, if you will just leave the bill for damages with Mrs. Jacques, her lawyer will take care of everything. You can even throw in ten per cent, for mental anguish."

Anna felt like clapping her hands in glee. The whole Security office was no match for this fiend.

"You're getting last night mixed up with the night before," snapped Martha Jacques. "You met Miss van Tuyl last night. You were with her several hours. Don't lie about it."

Again Ruy Jacques peered earnestly into Anna's face. He finally shook his head. "Last night? Well, I can't deny it. Guess you'll have to pay up, Martha. Her face *is* familiar, but I just can't remember what I did to make her mad. The bucket of paint and the slumming dowager was *last* week, wasn't it?"

Anna smiled. "You didn't injure me. We simply danced together on the square, that's all. I'm here at Mrs. Jacques' request." From the corner of her eye she watched Martha Jacques and the colonel exchange questioning glances, as if to say, "Perhaps there is really nothing between them."

But the scientist was not completely satisfied. She turned her eyes on her husband. "It's a strange coincidence that you should come just at this time. Exactly why *are* you here, if not to becloud the issue of this woman and your future psychiatrical treatment? Why don't you answer? What is the matter with you?"

For Ruy Jacques stood there, swaying like a stricken satyr, his eyes coals of pain in a face of anguished flames. He contorted backward once, as though attempting to placate furious fangs tearing at the hump on his back.

Anna leaped to catch him as he collapsed.

He lay cupped in her lap moaning voicelessly. Something in his hump, which lay against her left breast, seethed and raged like a genie locked in a bottle.

"Colonel Grade," said the psychiatrist quietly, "you will order an ambulance. I must analyze this pain syndrome at the clinic immediately."

Ruy Jacques was hers.

CHAPTER SIX

"THANKS awfully for coming, Matt," said Anna warmly.

"Glad to, honey." He looked down at the prone figure on the clinic cot. "How's our friend?"

"Still unconscious, and under general analgesic. I called you in because I want to air some ideas about this man that scare me when I think about them alone."

The psychogeneticist adjusted his spectacles with elaborate casualness. "Really? Then you think you've found what's wrong with him? Why he can't read or write?"

"Does it have to be something *wrong*?"

"What else would you call it? A . . . *gift*?"

She studied him narrowly. "I might—and you might—if he got something in return for his loss. That would depend on whether there was a net gain, wouldn't it? And don't pretend you don't know what I'm talking about. Let's get out in the open. You've known the Jacques—both of them—for years. You had me put on his case because you think he and I might find in the mind and body of the other a mutual solution to our identical aberrations. Well?"

Bell tapped imperturbably at his cigar. "As you say, the question is, whether he got enough in return—enough to compensate for his lost skills."

She gave him a baffled look. "All right, then, I'll do the

talking. Ruy Jacques opened Grade's private door, when Grade alone knew the combination. And when he got in the room with us, he knew what we had been talking about. It was just as though it had all been written out for him, somehow. You'd have thought the lock combination had been pasted on the door, and that he'd looked over a transcript of our conversation."

"Only, he can't read," observed Bell.

"You mean, he can't read . . . *writing*?"

"What else is there?"

"Possibly some sort of thought residuum . . . in *things*. Perhaps some message in the metal of Grade's door, and in certain objects in the room." She watched him closely. "I see you aren't surprised. You've known this all along."

"I admit nothing. You, on the other hand, must admit that your theory of thought-reading is superficially fantastic."

"So would writing be—to a Neanderthal cave dweller. But tell me, Matt, where do our thoughts go after we think them? What is the extra-cranial fate of those feeble, intricate electric oscillations we pick up on the encephalograph?. We know they can and do penetrate the skull, that they can pass through bone, like radio waves. Do they go on out into the universe forever? Or do dense substances like Grade's door eventually absorb them all? Do they set up their wispy patterns in metals, which then begin to vibrate in sympathy, like piano wires responding to a noise?"

Bell drew heavily on his cigar. "Seriously, I don't know. But I will say this: your theory is not inconsistent with certain psychogenetic predictions."

"Such as?"

"Eventual telemusical communication of all thought. The encephalograph, you know, looks oddly like a musical sound track. Oh, we can't expect to convert overnight to communication of pure thought by pure music. Naturally, crude transitional forms will intervene. But *any* type of direct idea transmission that involves the sending and receiving of rhythm and modulation as such is a cut higher than communication in a verbal medium, and may be a rudimentary step upward toward true musical communion, just as dawn man presaged true words with allusive, onomatapoeic monosyllables."

"There's your answer, then," said Anna. "Why should Ruy Jacques trouble to read, when every bit of metal around him is an open book?" She continued speculatively. "You might look at it this way. Our ancestors forgot how to swing through the trees when they learned how to walk erect. Their history is recapitulated in our very young. Almost immediately after birth, a human infant can hang by his hands, apelike. And then, after a week or so, he forgets what no human infant ever really needed to know. So now Ruy forgets how to read. A great pity. Perhaps. But if the world were peopled with Ruys, they wouldn't need to know how, for after the first few years of infancy, they'd learn to use their metal-empathic sense. They might even say, 'It's all very nice to be able to read and write and swing about in trees when you're *quite* young, but after all, one matures.' "

She pressed a button on the desk slide viewer that sat on a table by the artist's bed. "This is a radiographic slide of Ruy's cerebral hemispheres as viewed from above, probably old stuff to you. It shows that the 'horns' are not mere localized growths in the prefrontal area, but extend as slender tracts around the respective hemispheric peripheries to the visuo-sensory area of the occipital lobes, where they turn and enter the cerebral interior, there to merge in an enlarged ball-like juncture at a point over the cerebellum where the pineal 'eye', is ordinarily found."

"But the pineal is completely missing in the slide," demurred Bell.

"That's the question," countered Anna. "*Is* the pineal absent—or, are the 'horns' actually the pineal, enormously enlarged and bifurcated? I'm convinced that the latter is the fact. For reasons presently unknown to me, this heretofore small, obscure lobe has grown, bifurcated, and forced its destructive dual limbs not only through the soft cerebral tissue concerned with the ability to read, but also has gone on to skirt half the cerebral circumference to the forehead, where even the hard frontal bone of the skull has softened under its pressure." She looked at Bell closely. "I infer that it's just a question of time before I, too, forget how to read and write."

Bell's eyes drifted evasively to the immobile face of the unconscious artist. "But the number of neurons in a given mammalian brain remains constant after birth," he said.

"These cells can throw out numerous dendrites and create increasingly complex neural patterns as the subject grows older, but he can't grow any more of the primary neurons."

"I know. That's the trouble. Ruy can't grow more brain, but he has." She touched her own "horns" wonderingly. "And I guess I have, too. *What*——?"

Following Bell's glance, she bent over to inspect the artist's face, and started as from a physical blow.

Eyes like anguished talons were clutching hers.

His lips moved, and a harsh whisper swirled about her ears like a desolate wind: ". . . The Nightingale . . . in death . . . greater beauty unbearable . . . but *watch* . . . *THE ROSE!*"

White-faced, Anna staggered backwards through the door.

CHAPTER SEVEN

BELL'S hurried footsteps were just behind her as she burst into her office and collapsed on the consultation couch. Her eyes were shut tight, but over her labored breathing she heard the psychogeneticist sit down and leisurely light another cigar.

Finally she opened her eyes. "Even *you* found out something that time. There's no use asking me what he meant."

"Isn't there? Who will dance the part of The Student on opening night?"

"Ruy. Only, he will really do little beyond provide support to the prima ballerina, The Nightingale, that is, at the beginning and end of the ballet."

"And who plays The Nightingale?"

"Ruy hired a professional—La Tanid."

Bell blew a careless cloud of smoke toward the ceiling. "Are you sure *you* aren't going to take the part?"

"The role is strenuous in the extreme. For me, it would be a physical impossibility."

"Now."

"What do you mean—*now?*"

He looked at her sharply. "You know very well what I mean. You know it so well your whole body is quivering. Your ballet première is four weeks off—but you know and I know that Ruy has already seen it. Interesting." He tapped coolly at his cigar. *"Almost as interesting as your belief he saw you playing the part of The Nightingale."*

Anna clenched her fists. This must be faced rationally. She inhaled deeply, and slowly let her breath out. "How can even *he* see things that haven't happened yet?"

"I don't know for sure. But I can guess, and so could you if you'd calm down a bit. We do know that the pineal is a residuum of the single eye that our very remote seagoing ancestors had in the centre of their fishy foreheads. Suppose this fossil eye, now buried deep in the normal brain, were reactivated. What would we be able to see with it? Nothing spatial, nothing dependent on light stimuli. But let us approach the problem inductively. I shut one eye. The other can fix Anna van Tuyl in a depthless visual plane. But with two eyes I can follow you stereoscopically, as you move about in space. Thus, adding an eye adds a dimension. With the pineal as a third eye I should be able to follow you through time. So Ruy's awakened pineal should permit him at least a hazy glimpse of the future."

"What a marvellous—and terrible gift."

"But not without precedent," said Bell. "I suspect that a more or less reactivated pineal lies behind every case of clairvoyance collected in the annals of para-psychology. And I can think of at least one historical instance in which the pineal has actually tried to penetrate the forehead, though evidently only in monolobate form. All Buddhist statues carry a mark on the forehead symbolic of an 'inner eye'. From what we know now, Budda's 'inner eye' was something more than symbolic."

"Granted. But a time-sensitive pineal still doesn't explain the pain in Ruy's hump. Nor the hump itself, for that matter."

"What," said Bell, "makes you think the hump is anything more than what it seems—a spinal disease characterized by a growth of laminated tissue?"

"It's not that simple, and you know it. You're familiar

with 'phantom limb' cases, such as where the amputee retains an illusion of sensation or pain in the amputated hand or foot?"

He nodded.

She continued: "But you know, of course, that amputation isn't an absolute prerequisite to a 'phantom.' A child born armless may experience phantom limb sensations for years. Suppose such a child were thrust into some improbable armless society, and their psychiatrists tried to cast his sensory pattern into their own mould. How could the child explain to them the miracle of arms, hands, fingers—things of which he had occasional sensory intimations, but had never seen, and could hardly imagine? Ruy's case is analogous. He is four-limbed and presumably springs from normal stock. Hence the phantom sensations in his hump point toward a *potential* organ—a foreshadowing of the future, rather than toward memories of a limb once possessed. To use a brutish example, Ruy is like the tadpole rather than the snake. The snake had his legs briefly, during the evolutionary recapitulation of his embryo. The tadpole has yet to shed his tail and develop legs. But one might assume that each has some faint phantom sensoria of legs."

Bell appeared to consider this. "That still doesn't account for Ruy's pain. I wouldn't think the process of growing a tail would be painful for a tadpole, nor a phantom limb for Ruy—if it's inherent in his physical structure. But be that as it may, from all indications he is still going to be in considerable pain when that narcotic wears off. What are you going to do for him *then?* Section the ganglia leading to his hump?"

"Certainly not. Then he would *never* be able to grow that extra organ. Anyhow, even in normal phantom limb cases, cutting nerve tissue doesn't help. Excision of neuromas from limb stumps brings only temporary relief—and may actually aggravate a case of hyperaesthesia. No, phantom pain sensations are central rather then peripheral. However, as a temporary analgesic I shall try a two per cent solution of novocaine near the proper thoracic ganglia." She looked at her watch. "We'd better be getting back to him."

CHAPTER EIGHT

ANNA withdrew the syringe needle from the man's side and rubbed the last puncture with an alcoholic swab.

"How do you feel, Ruy?" asked Bell.

The woman stooped beside the sterile linens and looked at the face of the prone man. "He doesn't," she said uneasily. "He's out cold again."

"Really?" Bell bent over beside her and reached for the man's pulse. "But it was only two per cent novocaine. Most remarkable."

"I'll order a counter-stimulant," said Anna nervously. "I don't like this."

"Oh, come, girl. Relax. Pulse and respiration normal. In fact, I think you're nearer collapse than he. This is very interesting . . ." His voice trailed off in musing surmise. "Look, Anna, there's nothing to keep both of us here. He's in no danger whatever. I've got to run along. I'm sure you can attend to him."

I know, she thought. You want me to be alone with him.

She acknowledged his suggestion with a reluctant nod of her head, and the door closed behind his chuckle.

For some moments thereafter she studied in deep abstraction the regular rise and fall of the man's chest.

So Ruy Jacques had set another medical precedent. He'd received a local anaesthetic that should have done nothing more than desensitise the deformed growth in his back for an hour or two. But here he lay, in apparent coma, just as though under a general cerebral anaesthetic.

Her frown deepened.

X-ray plates had showed his dorsal growth simply as a compacted mass of cartilaginous laminated tissue (the same as hers) penetrated here and there by neural ganglia. In deadening those ganglia she should have accomplished nothing more than local anaesthetization of that tissue mass, in the same manner that one anaesthetizes an arm or leg by deadening the appropriate spinal ganglion. But the actual result was not local, but general. It was as though one had administered a mild local to the radial nerve of the forearm to deaden pain in the hand, but had instead anaesthetized the cerebrum.

And *that*, of course, was utterly senseless, completely incredible, because anaesthesia works from the higher neural centres down, not vice versa. Deadening a certain area of the parietal lobe could kill sensation in the radial nerve and the hand, but a hypo in the radial nerve wouldn't knock out the parietal lobe of the cerebrum, because the parietal organization was neurally superior. Analogously, anaesthetizing Ruy Jacques' hump shouldn't have deadened his entire cerebrum, because certainly his cerebrum was to be presumed neurally superior to that dorsal malformation.

To be presumed . . .

But with Ruy Jacques, presumptions were—invalid.

So *that* was what Bell had wanted her to discover. Like some sinister reptile of the Mesozoic, Ruy Jacques had *two* neural organizations, one in his skull and one on his back, the latter being superior to, and in some degree controlling, the one in his skull, just as the cerebral cortex in human beings and other higher animals assists and screens the work of the less intricate cerebellum, and just as the cerebellum governs the still more primitive medulla oblongata in the lower vertebrata, such as in frogs and fishes. In anaesthetizing his bump, she had disrupted communications in his highest centres of consciousness, and in anaesthetizing the higher, dorsal centre, she had apparently simultaneously deactivated his "normal" brain.

As full realization came, she grew aware of a curious numbness in her thighs, and of faint overtones of mingled terror and awe in the giddy throbbing in her forehead. Slowly, she sank into the bedside chair.

For as this man was, so must she become. The day lay ahead when *her* pineal growths must stretch to the point of disrupting the grey matter in her occipital lobes, and destroy her ability to read. And the time must come, too, when *her* dorsal growth would inflame her whole body with its anguished writhing, as it had done his, and try with probable equal futility to burst its bonds.

And all of this must come—soon; before her ballet première, certainly. The enigmatic skein of the future would be unravelled to her evolving intellect even as it now was to Ruy Jacques'. She could find all the answers she sought . . . Dream's end . . . the Nightingale's death song . . . The Rose. And she would find them whether she wanted to or not.

She groaned uneasily.

At the sound, the man's eyelids seemed to tremble; his breathing slowed momentarily, then became faster.

She considered this in perplexity. He was unconscious, certainly; yet he made definite responses to aural stimuli. Possibly she had anaesthetized neither member of the hypothetical brain-pair, but had merely cut, temporarily, their lines of intercommunication, just as one might temporarily disorganize the brain of a laboratory animal by anaesthetizing the pons Varolii linking the two cranial hemispheres.

Of one thing she was sure: Ruy Jacques, unconscious, and temporarily mentally disintegrate, was not going to conform to the behavior long standardized for other unconscious and disintegrate mammals. Always one step beyond what she ever expected. Beyond man. Beyond genius.

She arose quietly and tiptoed the short distance to the bed.

When her lips were a few inches from the artist's right ear, she said softly: "What is your name?"

The prone figure stirred uneasily. His eyelids fluttered, but did not open. His wine-colored lips parted, then shut, then opened again. His reply was a harsh, barely intelligible whisper: "Zhak."

"What are you doing?"

"Searching . . ."

"For what?"

"A red rose."

"There are many red roses."

Again his somnolent, metallic whisper: "No, there is but one."

She suddenly realized that her own voice was becoming tense, shrill. She forced it back into a lower pitch. "Think of that rose. Can you see it?"

"Yes . . . yes!"

She cried: *"What is the rose?"*

It seemed that the narrow walls of the room would clamour forever their outraged metallic modesty, if something hadn't frightened away their pain. Ruy Jacques opened his eyes and struggled to rise on one elbow.

On his sweating forehead was a deep frown. But his eyes were apparently focused on nothing in particular, and despite his seemingly purposive motor reaction, she knew that actually her question had but thrown him deeper into his strange spell.

Swaying a little on the dubious support of his right elbow, he muttered: "*You* are not the rose . . . not yet . . . not yet . . ."

She gazed at him in shocked stupor as his eyes closed slowly and he slumped back on the sheet. For a long moment there was no sound in the room but his deep and rhythmic breathing.

CHAPTER NINE

WITHOUT turning from her glum perusal of the clinic grounds framed in her window, Anna threw the statement over her shoulder as Bell entered the office. "Your friend Jacques refuses to return for a check-up. I haven't seen him since he walked out a week ago."

"Is that fatal?"

She turned blood-shot eyes on him. "Not to Ruy."

The man's expression twinkled. "He's your patient, isn't he? It's your duty to make a house call."

"I certainly shall. I was going to call him on the visor to make an appointment."

"He doesn't have a visor. Everybody just walks in. There's something doing in his studio nearly every night. If you're bashful, I'll be glad to take you."

"No thanks. I'll go alone—early."

Bell chuckled. "I'll see you tonight."

CHAPTER TEN

NUMBER 98, was a sad, ramshackled, four-storey, plaster-front affair, evidently thrown up during the materials shortage of the late forties.

Anna took a deep breath, ignored the unsteadiness of her knees, and climbed the half dozen steps of the front stoop.

There seemed to be no exterior bell. Perhaps it was inside. She pushed the door in and the waning evening light followed her into the hall. From somewhere came a frantic barking, which was immediately silenced.

Anna peered uneasily up the rickety stairs, then whirled as a door opened behind her.

A fuzzy canine muzzle thrust itself out of the crack in the doorway and growled cautiously. And in the same crack, farther up, a dark wrinkled face looked out at her suspiciously. "Whaddaya want?"

Anna retreated half a step. "Does he bite?"

"Who, Mozart? Nah, he couldn't dent a banana." The creature added with anile irrelevance. "Ruy gave him to me because Mozart's dog followed him to the grave."

"Then this is where Mr. Jacques lives?"

"Sure, fourth floor, but you're early." The door opened wider. "Say, haven't I seen you somewhere before?"

Recognition was simultaneous. It was that animated stack of purple dresses, the ancient vendress of love philters.

"Come in, dearie," purred the old one, "and I'll mix you up something special."

"Never mind," said Anna hurriedly. "I've got to see Mr. Jacques." She turned and ran toward the stairway.

A horrid floating cackle whipped and goaded her flight, until she stumbled out on the final landing and set up an insensate skirling on the first door she came to.

From within an irritated voice called: "Aren't you getting a little tired of that? Why don't you come in and rest your knuckles?"

"Oh." She felt faintly foolish. "It's me—Anna van Tuyl."

"Shall I take the door off its hinges, doctor?"

Anna turned the knob and stepped inside.

Ruy Jacques stood with his back to her, palette in hand, facing an easel bathed in the slanting shafts of the setting sun. He was apparently blocking in a caricature of a nude model lying, face averted, on a couch beyond the easel.

Anna felt a sharp pang of disappointment. She'd wanted him to herself a little while. Her glance flicked about the studio.

Framed canvases obscured by dust were stacked willy-nilly about the walls of the big room. Here and there were bits of statuary. Behind a nearby screen the disarray of a cot peeped out at her. Beyond the screen was a wire-phono. In the opposite wall was a door that evidently opened into the model's dressing alcove. In the opposite corner stood a battered electronic piano which she recognized as the Fourier audiosynthesizer type.

She gave an involuntary gasp as the figure of a man suddenly separated from the piano and bowed to her.

Colonel Grade.

So the lovely model with the invisible face must be—Martha Jacques.

There was no possibility of mistake, for now the model had turned her face a little, and acknowledged Anna's faltering stare with complacent mockery.

Of all evenings, why did Martha Jacques have to pick *this* one?

The artist faced the easel again. His harsh jeer floated back to the psychiatrist: "Behold the perfect female body!"

Perhaps it was the way he said this that saved her. She had a fleeting suspicion that he had recognized her disappointment, had anticipated the depths of her gathering despair, and had deliberately shaken her back into reality.

In a few words he had borne upon her the idea that his enormously complex mind contained neither love nor hate, even for his wife, and that while he found in her a physical perfection suitable for transference to canvas or marble, that nevertheless he writhed in a secret torment over this very perfection, as though in essence the

42

woman's physical beauty simply stated a lack he could not name, and might never know.

With a wary, futile motion he lay aside his brushes and palette. "Yes, Martha is perfect, physically and mentally, and knows it." He laughed brutally. "What she doesn't know, is that frozen beauty admits of no plastic play of meaning. There's nothing behind perfection, because it has no meaning but itself."

There was a clamour on the stairs. "Hah!" cried Jacques. "*More* early-comers. The word must have got around that Martha brought the liquor. School's out, Mart. Better hop into the alcove and get dressed."

Matthew Bell was among the early arrivals. His face lighted up when he saw Anna, then clouded when he picked out Grade and Martha Jacques.

Anna noticed that his mouth was twitching worriedly as he motioned to her.

"What's wrong?" she asked.

"Nothing—yet. But I wouldn't have let you come if I'd known *they'd* be here. Has Martha given you any trouble?"

"No. Why should she? I'm here ostensibly to observe Ruy in my professional capacity."

"You don't believe that, and if you get careless, *she* won't either. So watch your step with Ruy while Martha's around. And even when she's not around. Too many eyes here—Security men—Grade's crew. Just don't let Ruy involve you in anything that might attract attention. So much for that. Been here long?"

"I was the first guest—except for *her* and Grade."

"Hmm. I should have escorted you. Even though you're his psychiatrist, this sort of thing sets her to thinking."

"I can't see the harm of coming alone. It isn't as though Ruy were going to try to make love to me in front of all these people."

"That's exactly what it is as though!" He shook his head and looked about him. "Believe me, I know him better than you. The man is insane . . . unpredictable."

Anna felt a tingle of anticipation . . . or was it of apprehension? "I'll be careful," she said.

"Then come on. If I can get Martha and Ruy into one of their eternal Science-versus-Art arguments, I believe they'll forget about you."

CHAPTER ELEVEN

"I REPEAT," said Bell, "we are watching the germination of another Renaissance. The signs are unmistakable, and should be of great interest to practicing sociologists and policemen." He turned from the little group beginning to gather about him and beamed artlessly at the passing fate of Colonel Grade.

Grade paused. "And just what are the signs of a renaissance?" he demanded.

"Mainly climatic change and enormously increased leisure, Colonel. Either alone can make a big difference combined, the result is multiplicative rather than additive."

Anna watched Belle's eyes rove the room and join with those of Martha Jacques, as he continued: "Take temperature. In seven thousand B.C. *homo sapiens,* even in the Mediterranean area, was a shivering nomad; fifteen or twenty centuries later a climatic upheaval had turned Mesopotamia, Egypt and the Yangste valley into garden spots, and the first civilizations were born. Another warm period extending over several centuries and ending about twelve hundred A.D. launched the Italian Renaissance and the great Ottoman culture, before the temperature started falling again. Since the middle of the seventeenth century the mean temperature of New York City has been increasing at the rate of about one-tenth of a degree per year. In another century palm trees will be commonplace on Fifth Avenue." He broke off and bowed benignantly. "Hello, Mrs. Jacques. I was just mentioning that in past renaissances, mild climates and bounteous crops gave man leisure to think, and to create."

When the woman shrugged her shoulders and made a gesture as though to walk on, Bell continued hurriedly: "Yes, *those* renaissances gave us the Parthenon, *The Last*

Supper, the Taj Mahal. *Then,* the *artist* was supreme. But this time it might not happen that way, because we face a simultaneous technologic and climatic optimum. Atomic energy has virtually abolished labor as such, but without the international leavening of common art that united the first Egyptian, Sumerian, Chinese and Greek cities. Without pausing to consolidate his gains, the scientist rushes on to greater things, to Sciomnia, and to a Sciomnic power source"—he exchanged a sidelong look with the woman scientist—"a machine which, we are informed, may overnight fling man toward the nearer stars. When that day comes, the artist is through . . . unless . . ."

"Unless what?" asked Martha Jacques coldly.

"Unless this Renaissance, sharpened and intensified as it has been by its double maxima of climate and science, is able to force a response comparable to that of the Aurignacean Renaissance of twenty-five thousand B.C., to wit, the flowering of the Cro-Magnon, the first of the modern men. Wouldn't it be ironic if our greatest scientist solved Sciomnia, only to come a cropper at the hands of what may prove to be one of the first primitive specimens of *homo superior*—her husband?"

Anna watched with interest as the psychogeneticist smiled engagingly at Martha Jacques' frowning face, while at the same time he looked beyond her to catch the eye of Ruy Jacques, who was plinking in apparent aimlessness at the keyboard of the Fourier piano.

Martha Jacques said curtly: "I'm afraid, Dr. Bell, that I can't get too excited about your Renaissance. When you come right down to it, local humanity, whether dominated by art or science, is nothing but a temporary surface scum on a primitive backwoods planet."

Bell nodded blandly. "To most scientists Earth is admittedly commonplace. Psychogeneticists, on the other hand, consider this planet and its people one of the wonders of the universe."

"Really?" asked Grade. "And just what have we got here that they don't have on Betelgeuse?"

"Three things," replied Bell. "One—Earth's atmosphere has enough carbon dioxide to grow the forest-spawning grounds of man's primate ancestors, thereby ensuring an unspecialized, quasi-erect, manually-activated species capable of indefinite psychophysical development.

It might take the saurian life of a desert planet another billion years to evolve an equal physical and mental structure. Two—that same atmosphere had a surface pressure of 760 mm. of mercury and a mean temperature of about 25 degrees Centigrade—excellent conditions for the transmission of sound, speech, and song; and those early men took to it like a duck to water. Compare the difficulty of communication by direct touching of antennae, as the arthropodic pseudo-homindal citizens of certain airless worlds must do. Three—the solar spectrum within its very short frequency range of 760 to 390 millimicrons offers seven colors of remarkable variety and contrast, which our ancestors quickly made their own. From the beginning, they could see that they moved in multichrome beauty. Consider the ultra-sophisticate dwelling in a dying sun system—and pity him for he can see only red and a little infra red."

"If that's the only difference," snorted Grade, "I'd say you psychogeneticists were getting worked up over nothing."

Bell smiled past him at the approaching figure of Ruy Jacques. "You may be right, of course, Colonel, but I think you're missing the point. To the psychogeneticist it appears that terrestrial environment is promoting the evolution of a most extraordinary being—a type of *homo* whose energies beyond the barest necessities are devoted to strange, unproductive activities. And to what end? We don't know—yet. But we can guess. Give a psychogeneticist Eohippus and the grassy plains, and he'd predict the modern horse. Give him archeopteryx and a dense atmosphere, and he could imagine the swan. Give him *h. sapiens* and a two-day work week, or better yet, Ruy Jacques and a no-day work week, and what will he predict?"

"The poorhouse?" asked Jacques, sorrowfully.

Bell laughed. "Not quite. An evolutionary spurt, rather. As *sapiens* turns more and more into his abstract world of the arts, music in particular, the psychogeneticist foresees increased communication in terms of music. This might require certain cerebral realignments in *sapiens,* and perhaps the development of special membranous neural organs—which in turn might lead to completely new mental and physical abilities, and the conquest of new dimensions—just as the human tongue eventually developed from a tasting organ into a means of long distance vocal communication."

"Not even in Ruy's Science/Art diatribes," said Mrs. Jacques, "have I heard greater nonsense. If this planet is to have any future worthy of the name, you can be sure it will be through the leadership of her scientists."

"I wouldn't be too sure," countered Bell. "The artist's place in society has advanced tremendously in the past half-century. And I mean the minor artist—who is identified simply by his profession and not by any exceptional reputation. In our own time we have seen the financier forced to extend social equality to the scientist. And today the palette and musical sketch pad are gradually toppling the test tube and the cyclotron from their pedestals. In the first Renaissance the merchant and soldier inherited the ruins of church and feudal empire; in this one we peer through the crumbling walls of capitalism and nationalism and see the artist . . . or the scientist . . . ready to emerge as the cream of society. The question is, *which one?*"

"For the sake of law and order," declared Colonel Grade, "it must be the scientist, working in the defence of his country. Think of the military insecurity of an art-dominated society. If——"

Ruy Jacques broke in: "There is only one point on which I must disagree with you." He turned a disarming smile on his wife. "I really don't see how the scientist fits into the picture at all. Do you, Martha? For the artist is *already* supreme. He dominates the scientist, and if he likes, he is perfectly able to draw upon his more sensitive intuition for those various restatements of artistic principles that the scientists are forever trying to fob off on a decreasingly gullible public under the guise of novel scientific laws. I say that the artist is aware of those 'new' laws long before the scientist, and has the option of presenting them to the public in a pleasing art form or as a dry, abstruse equation. He may, like da Vinci, express his discovery of a beautiful curve in the form of a breath-taking spiral staircase in a *château* at Blois, or, like Dürer, he may analyze the curve mathematically and announce its logarithmic formula. In either event he anticipates Descartes, who was the first mathematician to rediscover the logarithmic spiral."

The woman laughed grimly. "All right. *You're* an artist. Just what scientific law have *you* discovered?"

"I have discovered," answered the artist with calm pride, "what will go down in history as 'Jacques' Law of Stellar Radiation'."

Anna and Bell exchanged glances. The older man's look of relief said plainly: "The battle is joined; they'll forget you."

Martha Jacques peered at the artist suspiciously. Anna could see that the woman was genuinely curious but caught between her desire to crush, to damn any such amateurish "discovery" and her fear that she was being led into a trap. Anna herself, after studying the exaggerated innocence of the man's wide, unblinking eyes knew immediately that he was subtly enticing the woman out on the rotten limb of her own dry perfection.

In near-hypnosis Anna watched the man draw a sheet of paper from his pocket. She marvelled at the superb blend of diffidence and braggadocio with which he unfolded it and handed it to the woman scientist.

"Since I can't write, I had one of the fellows write it down for me, but I think he got it right," he explained. "As you see, it boils down to seven prime equations."

Anna watched a puzzled frown steal over the woman's brow. "But each of these equations expands into hundreds more, especially the seventh, which is the longest of them all." The frown deepened. "Very interesting. Already I see hints of the Russell diagram . . ."

The man started. "What! H. N. Russell, who classified stars into spectral classes? You mean he scooped me?"

"Only if your work is accurate, which I doubt."

The artist stammered: "But——"

"And here," she continued in crisp condemnation, "is nothing more than a restatement of the law of light-pencil wavering, which explains why stars twinkle and planets don't, and which has been known for two hundred years."

Ruy Jacques' face lengthened lugubriously.

The woman smiled grimly and pointed. "These parameters are just a poor approximation of the Bethe law of nuclear fission in stars—old since the thirties."

The man stared at the scathing finger. "Old . . . ?"

"I fear so. But still not bad for an amateur. If you kept at this sort of thing all your life, you might eventually develop something novel. But this is a mere hodge-podge, a rehash of material any real scientist learned in his teens."

"But Martha," pleaded the artist, "surely it isn't *all* old?"

"I can't say with certainty, of course," returned the woman with malice-edged pleasure, "until I examine every sub-equation. I can only say that, fundamentally, scientists long ago anticipated the artist, represented by the great Ruy Jacques. In the aggregate, your amazing Law of Stellar Radiation has been known for two hundred years or more."

Even as the man stood there, as though momentarily stunned by the enormity of his defeat, Anna began to pity his wife.

The artist shrugged his shoulders wistfully. "Science versus Art. So the artist has given his all, and lost. Jacques' Law must sing its swan song, then be forever forgotten." He lifted a resigned face toward the scientist. "Would you, my dear, administer the *coup de grâce* by setting up the proper co-ordinates in the Fourier audiosynthesizer?"

Anna wanted to lift a warning hand, cry out to the man that he was going too far, that the humiliation he was preparing for his wife was unnecessary, unjust, and would but thicken the wall of hatred that cemented their antipodal souls together.

But it was too late. Martha Jacques was already walking toward the Fourier piano, and within seconds had set up the polar-defined data and had flipped the toggle switch. The psychiatrist found her mind and tongue to be literally paralyzed by the swift movement of this unwitting drama, which was now toppling over the brink of its tragicomic climax.

A deep silence fell over the room.

Anna caught an impression of avid faces, most of whom—Jacques' most intimate friends—would understand the nature of his little playlet and would rub salt into the abraded wound he was delivering his wife.

Then in the space of three seconds, it was over.

The Fourier-piano had synthesized the seven equations, six short, one long, into their tonal equivalents, and it was over.

Dorran, the orchestra leader, broke the uneasy stillness that followed. "I say, Ruy old chap," he blurted, "just what is the difference in 'Jacques' Law of Stellar Radiation' and 'Twinkle, twinkle, little star'?"

Anna, in mingled amusement and sympathy, watched the face of Martha Jacques slowly turn crimson.

The artist replied in amazement. "Why, now that you mention it, there does seem to be a little resemblance."

"It's a dead ringer!" cried a voice.

" 'Twinkle, twinkle' is an old continental folk tune," volunteered another. "I once traced it from Haydn's 'Surprise Symphony' back to the fourteenth century."

"Oh, but that's quite impossible," protested Jacques. "Martha has just stated that science discovered it first, only two hundred years ago."

The woman's voice dripped *aqua regia*. "You planned this deliberately, just to humiliate me in front of these . . . these clowns."

"Martha, I assure you . . . !"

"I'm warning you for the last time, Ruy. If you ever again humiliate me, I'll probably kill you!"

Jacques backed away in mock alarm until he was swallowed up in a swirl of laughter.

The group broke up, leaving the two women alone. Suddenly aware of Martha Jacques' bitter scrutiny, Anna flushed and turned toward her.

Martha Jacques said: "Why can't you make him come to his senses? I'm paying you enough."

Anna gave her a slow wry smile. "Then I'll need your help. And you aren't helping when you deprecate his sense of values—odd though they may seem to you."

"But Art is really so *foolish*! Science——"

Anna laughed shortly. "You see? Do you wonder he avoids you?"

"What would *you* do?"

"*I?*" Anna swallowed dryly.

Martha Jacques was watching her with narrowed eyes. "Yes, you. *If you wanted him?*"

Anna hesitated, breathing uneasily. Then gradually her eyes widened, became dreamy and full, like moons rising over the edge of some unknown, exotic land. Her lips opened with a nerveless fatalism. She didn't care what she said:

"I'd forget that I want, above all things, to be beautiful. I would think only of him. I'd wonder what he's thinking, and I'd forsake my mental integrity and try to think as he thinks. I'd learn to see through his eyes, and to hear through his ears. I'd sing over his successes, and hold my tongue when he failed. When he's moody and depressed, I wouldn't probe or insist that-I-could-help-you-if-you'd-only-let-me. Then—"

Martha Jacques snorted. "In short, you'd be nothing but a selfless shadow, devoid of personality or any mind or individuality of your own. That might be all right for one of your type. But for a scientist, the very thought is ridiculous!"

The psychiatrist lifted her shoulders delicately. "I agree. It *is* ridiculous. What *sane* woman at the peak of her profession would suddenly toss up her career to merge —you'd say 'submerge'—her identity, her very existence, with that of an utterly alien male mentality?"

"What woman, indeed?"

Anna mused to herself, and did not answer. Finally she said: "And yet, that's the price; take it or leave it, they say. What's a girl to do?"

"Stick up for her rights!" declared Martha Jacques spiritedly.

"All hail to unrewarding perseverance!" Ruy Jacques was back, swaying slightly. He pointed his half-filled glass toward the ceiling and shouted: "Friends! A toast! Let us drink to the two charter members of the Knights of the Crimson Grail." He bowed in saturnine mockery to his glowering wife. "To Martha! May she soon solve the Jacques Rosette and blast humanity into the heavens!"

Simultaneously he drank and held up a hand to silence the sudden spate of jeers and laughter. Then, turning toward the now apprehensive psychiatrist, he essayed a second bow of such sweeping grandiosity that his glass was upset. As he straightened, however, he calmly traded glasses with her. "To my old schoolteacher, Dr. van Tuyl. A nightingale whose secret ambition is to become as beautiful as a red red red rose. May Allah grant her prayers." He blinked at her beatifically in a sudden silence. "What was that comment, doctor?"

"I said you were a drunken idiot," replied Anna. "But let it pass." She was panting, her head whirling. She raised her voice to the growing cluster of faces. "Ladies and gentlemen, I offer you the third seeker of the grail! A truly great artist. Ruy Jacques, a child of the coming epoch, whose sole aim is not aimlessness, as he would like you to think, but a certain marvellous rose. Her curling petals shall be of subtle texture, yet firm withal, and brilliant red. It is this rose that he must find, to save his mind and body, and to put a soul in him."

"She's right!" cried the artist in dark glee. "To Ruy Jacques, then! Join in, everybody. The party's on Martha!"

He downed his glass, then turned a suddenly grave face to his audience. "But it's really such a pity in Anna's case, isn't it? Because her cure is so simple."

The psychiatrist listened; her head was throbbing dizzily.

"As any *competent* psychiatrist could tell her," continued the artist mercilessly, "she has identified herself with the nightingale in her ballet. The nightingale isn't much to look at. On top it's a dirty brown; at bottom, you might say it's a drab grey. But ah! The soul of this plain little bird! Look into my soul, she pleads. Hold me in your strong arms, look into my soul, and think me as lovely as a red rose."

Even before he put his wine glass down on the table, Anna knew what was coming. She didn't need to watch the stiffening cheeks and flaring nostrils of Martha Jacques, nor the sudden flash of fear in Bell's eyes, to know what was going to happen next.

He held out his arms to her, his swart satyr-face nearly impassive save for its eternal suggestion of sardonic mockery.

"You're right," she whispered, half to him, half to some other part of her, listening, watching. "I *do* want you to hold me in your arms and think me beautiful. But you can't, because you don't love me. It won't work. Not yet. Here, I'll prove it.

As from miles and centuries away, she heard Grade's horrified gurgle.

But her trance held. She entered the embrace of Ruy Jacques, and held her face up to his as much as her spine would permit, and closed her eyes.

He kissed her quickly on the forehead and released her. "There! Cured!"

She stood back and surveyed him thoughtfully. "I wanted you to see for yourself, that nothing can be beautiful to you—at least not until you learn to regard someone else as highly as you do Ruy Jacques."

Bell had drawn close. His face was wet, grey. He whispered: "Are you two insane? Couldn't you save this sort of thing for a less crowded occasion?"

But Anna was rolling rudderless in a fatalistic calm. "I had to show him something. Here. Now. He might never have tried it if he hadn't had an audience. Can you take me home now?"

"Worst thing possible," replied Bell agitatedly. "That'd just confirm Martha's suspicions." He looked around nervously. "She's gone. Don't know whether that's good or bad. But Grade's watching us. Ruy, if you've got the faintest intimations of decency, you'll wander over to that group of ladies and kiss a few of them. May throw Martha off the scent. Anna, you stay here. Keep talking. Try to toss it off as an amusing incident." He gave a short strained laugh. "Otherwise you're going to wind up as the First Martyr in the Cause of Art."

"I beg your pardon, Dr. van Tuyl."

It was Grade. His voice was brutally cold, and the syllables were clipped from his lips with a spine-tingling finality.

"Yes, Colonel?" said Anna nervously.

"The Security Bureau would like to ask you a few questions."

"Yes?"

Grade turned and stared icily at Bell. "It is preferred that the interrogation be conducted in private. It should not take long. If the lady would kindly step into the model's dressing room, my assistant will take over from there."

"Dr. van Tuyl was just leaving," said Bell huskily. "Did you have a coat, Anna?"

With a smooth unobtrusive motion Grade unsnapped the guard on his hip holster. "If Dr. van Tuyl leaves the dressing room within ten minutes, alone, she may depart from the studio in any manner she pleases."

Anna watched her friend's face become even paler. He wet his lips, then whispered. "I think you'd better go, Anna. Be careful."

CHAPTER TWELVE

THE room was small and nearly bare. Its sole furnishings were an ancient calendar, a clothes tree, a few stacks of dusty books, a table (bare save for a roll of canvas patching tape) and three chairs.

In one of the chairs, across the table, sat Martha Jacques.

She seemed almost to smile at Anna; but the amused curl of her beautiful lips was totally belied by her eyes, which pulsed hate with the paralyzing force of physical blows.

In the other chair sat Willie the Cork, almost unrecognizable in his groomed neatness.

The psychiatrist brought her hand to her throat as though to restore her voice, and at the movement, she saw from the corner of her eye that Willie, in a lightning motion, had simultaneously thrust his hand into his coat pocket, invisible below the table. She slowly understood that he held a gun on her.

The man was the first to speak, and his voice was so crisp and incisive that she doubted her first intuitive recognition. "Obviously, I shall kill you if you attempt any unwise action. So please sit down, Dr. van Tuyl. Let us put our cards on the table."

It was too incredible, too unreal, to arouse any immediate sense of fear. In numb amazement she pulled out the chair and sat down.

"As you may have suspected for some time," continued the man curtly, "I am a Security agent."

Anna found her voice. "I know only that I am being forcibly detained. What do you want?"

"Information, doctor. What government do you represent?"

"None."

The man fairly purred. "Don't you realize, doctor, that

as soon as you cease to answer responsively, I shall kill you?"

Anna van Tuyl looked from the man to the woman. She thought of circling hawks, and felt the intimations of terror. What could she have done to attract such wrathful attention? She didn't know. But then, *they* couldn't be sure about *her*, either. This man didn't want to kill her until he found out more. And by that time surely he'd see that it was all a mistake.

She said: "Either I am a psychiatrist attending a special case, or I am not. I am in no position to prove the positive. Yet, by syllogistic law, you must accept it as a possibility until you prove the negative. Therefore, until you have given me an opportunity to explain or disprove any evidence to the contrary, you can never be certain in your own mind that I am other than what I claim to be."

The man smiled, almost genially. "Well put, doctor. I hope they've been paying you what you are worth." He bent forward suddenly. "Why are you trying to make Ruy Jacques fall in love with you?"

She stared back with widening eyes. "What did you say?"

"Why are you trying to make Ruy Jacques fall in love with you?"

She could meet his eyes squarely enough, but her voice was now very faint: "I didn't understand you at first. You said . . . that I'm trying to make him fall in love with me." She pondered this for a long wondering moment, as though the idea were utterly new. "And I guess . . . it's true."

The man looked blank, then smiled with sudden appreciation. "You *are* clever. Certainly, you're the first to try *that* line. Though I don't know what you expect to gain with your false candour."

"False? Didn't you mean it yourself? No, I see you didn't. But Mrs. Jacques does. And she hates me for it. But I'm just part of the bigger hate she keeps for *him*. Even her Sciomnia equation is just part of that hate. She isn't working on a biophysical weapon just because she's a patriot, but more to spite him, to show him that her science is superior to——"

Martha Jacques' hand lashed viciously across the little table and struck Anna in the mouth.

The man merely murmured: "Please control yourself a bit longer, Mrs. Jacques. Interruptions from outside would be most inconvenient at this point." His humorless eyes returned to Anna. "One evening a week ago, when Mr. Jacques was under your care at the clinic, you left stylus and paper with him."

Anna nodded. "I wanted him to attempt automatic writing."

"What is 'automatic writing'?"

"Simply writing done while the conscious mind is absorbed in a completely extraneous activity, such as music. Mr. Jacques was to focus his attention on certain music composed by me while holding stylus and paper in his lap. If his recent inability to read and write was caused by some psychic block, it was quite possible that his subconscious mind might bypass the block, and he would write—just as one 'doodles' unconsciously when talking over the visor."

He thrust a sheet of paper at her. "Can you identify this?"

What was he driving at? She examined the sheet hesitantly. "It's just a blank sheet from my private monogrammed stationery. Where did you get it?"

"From the pad you left with Mr. Jacques."

"So?"

"We also found another sheet from the same pad under Mr. Jacques' bed. It had some interesting writing on it."

"But Mr. Jacques personally reported nil results."

"He was probably right."

"But you said he wrote something?" she insisted; momentarily her personal danger faded before her professional interest.

"I didn't say *he* wrote anything."

"Wasn't it written with that same stylus?"

"It was. But I don't think he wrote it. It wasn't in his handwriting."

"That's often the case in automatic writing. The script is modified according to the personality of the dissociated subconscious unit. The alteration is sometimes so great as to be unrecognizable as the handwriting of the subject."

He peered at her keenly. "This script was perfectly recognizable, Dr. van Tuyl. I'm afraid you've made a grave blunder. Now, shall I tell you in *whose* handwriting?"

She listened to her own whisper: "Mine?"

"Yes."

"What does it say?"

"You know very well."

"But I don't." Her underclothing was sticking to her body with a damp clammy feeling. "At least you ought to give me a chance to explain it. May I see it?"

He regarded her thoughtfully for a moment, then reached into his pocket sheaf. "Here's an electrostat. The paper, texture, ink, everything, is a perfect copy of your original."

She studied the sheet with a puzzled frown. There were a few lines of scribblings in purple. But it *wasn't* in her handwriting. In fact, it wasn't even handwriting—just a mass of illegible scrawls!

Anna felt a thrill of fear. She stammered: "What are you trying to do?"

"You don't deny you wrote it?"

"Of course I deny it." She could no longer control the quaver in her voice. Her lips were leaden masses, her tongue a stone slab. "It's—unrecognizable . . ."

The Cork floated with sinister patience. "In the upper left hand corner is your monogram: 'A.vT.', the same as on the first sheet. You will admit that, at least?"

For the first time, Anna really examined the presumed trio of initials enclosed in the familiar ellipse. The ellipse was there. But the print within it was—gibberish. She seized again at the first sheet—the blank one. The feel of the paper, even the smell, stamped it as genuine. It had been hers. But the monogram! "Oh no!" she whispered.

Her panic-stricken eyes flailed about the room. The calendar . . . same picture of the same cow . . . *but the rest* . . . ! A stack of books in the corner . . . titled in gold leaf . . . gathering dust for months . . . the label on the roll of patching tape on the table . . . even the watch on her wrist.

Gibberish. She could no longer read. She had forgotten how. Her ironic gods had chosen this critical moment to blind her with their brilliant bounty.

Then take it! And play for time!

She wet trembling lips. "I'm unable to read. My reading

glasses are in my bag, outside." She returned the script. "If *you'd* read it, I might recognize the contents."

The man said: "I thought you might try this, just to get my eyes off you. If you don't mind, I'll quote from memory:

" '——what a queer climax for the Dream! Yet, inevitable. Art versus Science decrees that one of us must destroy the Sciomniac weapon; but that could wait until we become more numerous. So, what I do is for him alone, and his future depends on appreciating it. Thus, Science bows to Art, but even Art isn't all. The Student must know the one greater thing when he sees the Nightingale dead, for only then will he recognize . . .' "

He paused.

"Is that all?" asked Anna.

"That's all."

"Nothing about a . . . rose?"

"No. What is 'rose' a code word for?"

Death? mused Anna. Was the rose a cryptolalic synonym for the grave? She closed her eyes and shivered. Were those really *her* thoughts, impressed into the mind and wrist of Ruy Jacques from some grandstand seat at her own ballet three weeks hence? But after all, why was it so impossible? Coleridge claimed *Kublai Khan* had been dictated to him through automatic writing. And that English mystic, William Blake, freely acknowledged being the frequent amanuensis for an unseen personality. And there were numerous other cases. So, from some unseen time and place, the mind of Anna van Tuyl had been attuned to that of Ruy Jacques, and his mind had momentarily forgotten that both of them could no longer write, and had recorded a strange reverie.

It was then that she noticed the—whispers.

No—not whispers—not exactly. More like rippling vibrations, mingling, rising, falling. Her heart beats quickened when she realized that their eerie pattern was soundless. It was as though something in her mind was suddenly vibrating *en rapport* with a subetheric world. Messages were beating at her for which she had no tongue or ear; they were beyond sound—beyond knowledge, and they swarmed dizzily around her from all directions. From the ring she wore. From the bronze buttons of her jacket.

From the vertical steam piping in the corner. From the metal reflector of the ceiling light.

And the strongest and most meaningful of all showered steadily from the invisible weapon. The Cork grasped in his coat pocket. Just as surely as though she had seen it done, she knew that the weapon had killed in the past. And not just once. She found herself attempting to unravel those thought residues of death—once—twice—three times . . . beyond which they faded away into steady, indecipherable time-muted violence.

And now that gun began to scream: "Kill! Kill! Kill!"

She passed her palm over her forehead. Her whole face was cold and wet. She swallowed noisily.

CHAPTER THIRTEEN

RUY JACQUES sat before the metal illuminator near his easel, apparently absorbed in the profound contemplation of his goatish features, and oblivious to the mounting gaiety about him. In reality he was almost completely lost in a soundless, sardonic glee over the triangular death-struggle that was nearing its climax beyond the inner wall of his studio, and which was magnified in his remarkable mind to an incredible degree by the paraboloid mirror of the illuminator.

Bell's low urgent voice began hacking at him again. "Her blood will be on your head. All you need to do is to go in there. Your wife wouldn't permit any shooting with you around."

The artist twitched his misshapen shoulders irritably. "*Maybe*. But why should I risk my skin for a silly little nightingale?"

"Can it be that your growth beyond *sapiens* has served simply to sharpen your objectivity, to accentuate your inherent egregious want of identity with even the best of your fellow creatures? Is the indifference that has driven

Martha nearly insane in a bare decade now too ingrained to respond to the first known female of your own unique breed?" Bell sighed heavily. "You don't have to answer. The very senselessness of her impending murder amuses you. Your nightingale is about to be impaled on her thorn—for nothing—as always. Your sole regret at the moment is that you can't twit her with the assurance that you will study her corpse diligently to find there the rose you seek."

"Such unfeeling heartlessness," said Jacques in regretful agreement, "is only to be expected in one of Martha's blunderings. I mean The Cork, of course. Doesn't he realize that Anna hasn't finished the score of her ballet? Evidently has no musical sense at all. I'll bet he was even turned down for the policemen's charity quarter. You're right, as usual, doc. We must punish such philistinism." He tugged at his chin, then rose from the folding stool.

"What are you going to do?" demanded the other sharply.

The artist weaved toward the phono cabinet. "Play a certain selection from Tchaikovsky's *Sixth*. If Anna's half the girl you think, she and Peter Ilyitch will soon have Mart eating out of their hands."

Bell watching him in anxious, yet half-trusting frustration as the other selected a spool from his library of electronic recordings and inserted it into the playback sprocket. In mounting mystification, he saw Jacques turn up the volume control as far as it would go.

CHAPTER FOURTEEN

MURDER, a one-act play directed by Mrs. Jacques, thought Anna. With sound effects by Mr. Jacques. But the facts didn't fit. It was unthinkable that Ruy would do anything to accommodate his wife. If anything, he would try to thwart Martha. But what was his purpose in starting off in the finale of the first movement of the *Sixth*? Was there some message there that he was trying to get across to her?

There was. She had it. She was going to live. If——

"In a moment," she told The Cork in a tight voice, "you are going to snap off the safety catch of your pistol, revise slightly your estimated line of fire, and squeeze the trigger. Ordinarily you could accomplish all three acts in almost instantaneous sequence. At the present moment, if I tried to turn the table over on you, you could put a bullet in my head before I could get well started. But in another sixty seconds you will no longer have that advantage, because your motor nervous system will be laboring under the superimposed pattern of the extraordinary Second Movement of the symphony that we now hear from the studio."

The Cork started to smile, then he frowned faintly. "What do you mean?"

"All motor acts are carried out in simple rhythmic patterns. We walk in the two-four time of the march. We waltz, use a pickaxe, and manually grasp or replace objects in three-four rhythm."

"This nonsense is purely a play for time," interjected Martha Jacques. "Kill her."

"It is a fact," continued Anna hurriedly. (Would that Second Movement never begin?) "A decade ago, when there were still a few factories using hand-assembly methods, the workmen speeded their work by breaking down the task into these same elemental rhythms, aided by appropriate music." (There! It was beginning! The immortal genius of that suicidal Russian was reaching across a century to save her!) "It so happens that the music you are hearing *now* is the Second Movement that I mentioned, and it's neither two-four nor three-four but *five*-four, an oriental rhythm that gives difficulty even to skilled occidental musicians and dancers. Subconsciously you are going to try to break it down into the only rhythms to which your motor nervous system is attuned. But you can't. Nor can *any* occidental, even a professional dancer, unless he has had special training"—her voice wobbled slightly—"in Delcrozian eurhythmics."

She crashed into the table.

Even though she had known that this must happen, her success was so complete, so overwhelming, that it momentarily appalled her.

Martha Jacques and The Cork had moved with anxious, rapid jerks, like puppets in a nightmare. But their rhythm was all wrong. With their ingrained four-time motor responses strangely modulated by a five-time pattern, the result was inevitably the arithmetical composite of the two: a neural beat, which could activate muscle tissue only when the two rhythms were in phase.

The Cork had hardly begun his frantic, spasmodic squeeze of the trigger when the careening table knocked him backward to the floor, stunned, beside Martha Jacques. It required but an instant for Anna to scurry around and extract the pistol from his numbed fist.

Then she pointed the trembling gun in the general direction of the carnage she had wrought and fought an urge to collapse against the wall.

She waited for the room to stop spinning, for the white, glass-eyed face of Martha Jacques to come into focus against the fuzzy background of the cheap paint-daubed rug. And then the eyes of the woman scientists flickered and closed.

With a wary glance at the weapon muzzle, The Cork gingerly pulled a leg from beneath the table edge: "You have the gun," he said softly. "You can't object if I assist Mrs. Jacques?"

"I *do* object," said Anna faintly. "She's merely unconscious . . . feels nothing. I want her to stay that way for a few minutes. If you approach her or make any unnecessary noise, I will probably kill you. So—both of you must stay here until Grade investigates. I know you have a pair of handcuffs. I'll give you ten seconds to lock yourself to that steam pipe in the corner—hands *behind* you, please."

She retrieved the roll of adhesive patching tape from the floor and fixed several strips across the agent's lips, following with a few swift loops around the ankles to prevent him stamping his feet.

A moment later, her face a damp mask, she closed the door leisurely behind her and stood there, breathing deeply and searching the room for Grade.

He was standing by the studio entrance, staring at her fixedly. When she favored him with a glassy smile, he simply shrugged his shoulders and began walking slowly toward her.

In growing panic her eyes darted about the room. Bell and Ruy Jacques were leaning over the phono, apparently deeply absorbed in the racing clangor of the music. She saw Bell nod a covert signal in her direction, but without looking directly at her. She tried not to seem hurried as she strolled over to join them. She knew that Grade was now walking toward them and was but a few steps away when Bell lifted his head and smiled.

"Everything all right?" said the psychogeneticist loudly.

She replied clearly: "Fine. Mrs. Jacques and a Security man just wanted to ask some questions." She drew in closer. Her lips framed a question to Bell: "Can Grade hear?"

Bell's lips formed a soft, nervous guttural: "No. He's moving off toward the dressing room door. If what I suspect happened behind that door is true, you have about ten seconds to get out of here. And then you've got to hide." He turned abruptly to the artist. "Ruy, you've got to take her down into the Via. Right now—*immediately*. Watch your opportunity and lose her when no one is looking. It shouldn't be too hard in that mob."

Jacques shook his head doubtfully. "Martha isn't going to like this. You know how strict she is on etiquette. I think there's a very firm statement in Emily Post that the host should never, never, *never* walk out on his guests before locking up the liquor and silverware. Oh, well, if you insist."

CHAPTER FIFTEEN

"TELL ya what the professor's gonna do, ladies and gentlemen. He's gonna defend not just one paradox. Not just two. But seventeen! In the space of one short hour, and without repeating himself, and including one he just thought up five minutes ago: 'Security is dangerous.'"

Ruy frowned, then whispered to Anna: "That was for

us. He means Security men are circulating. Let's move on. Next door. They won't look for a woman there."

Already he was pulling her away toward the chess parlor. They both ducked under the For Men Only sign (which she could no longer read), pushed through the bat-wing doors, and walked unobtrusively down between the wall and a row of players. One man looked up briefly out of the corner of his eye as they passed.

The woman paused uneasily. She had sensed the nervousness of the barker even before Ruy, and now still fainter impressions were beginning to ripple over the straining surface of her mind. They were coming from that chess player: from the coins in his pocket; from the lead weights of his chess pieces; and especially from the weapon concealed somewhere on him. The resonant histories of the chess pieces and coins she ignored. They held the encephalographic residua of too many minds. The invisible gun was clearer. There was something abrupt and violent, alternating with a more subtle, restrained rhythm. She put her hand to her throat as she considered one interpretation: *Kill—but wait.* Obviously, he'd dare not fire with Ruy so close.

"Rather warm here, too," murmured the artist. "Out we go."

As they stepped out into the street again, she looked behind her and saw that the man's chair was empty.

She held the artist's hand and pushed and jabbed after him, deeper into the revelling sea of humanity.

She ought to be thinking of ways to hide, of ways to use her new sensory gift. But another, more imperative train of thought continually clamored at her, until finally she yielded to a gloomy brooding.

Well, it was true. She wanted to be loved, and she wanted Ruy to love her. And he knew it. Every bit of metal on her shrieked her need for his love.

But—was she ready to love him? No! How could she love a man who lived only to paint that mysterious unpaintable scene of the nightingale's death, and who loved only himself? He was fascinating, but what sensible woman would wreck her career for such unilateral fascination? Perhaps Martha Jacques was right, after all.

"So you got him, after all!"

Anna whirled toward the crazy crackle, nearly jerking her hand from Ruy's grasp.

The vendress of love-philters stood leaning against the front centre pole of her tent, grinning toothily at Anna.

While the young woman stared dazedly at her, Jacques spoke up crisply: "Any strange men been around, Violet?"

"Why Ruy," she replied archly, "I think you're jealous. What kind of men?"

"Not the kind that haul you off to the alcoholic ward on Saturday nights. Not city dicks. Security men—quiet——seem slow, but really fast—see everybody—everything."

"Oh, *them*. Three went down the street two minutes ahead of you."

He rubbed his chin. "That's not so good. They'll start at that end of the Via and work up toward us until they meet the patrol behind us."

"Like grains of wheat between the millstones," cackled the crone. "*I knew* you'd turn to crime, sooner or later, Ruy. You were the only tenant I had who paid the rent regular."

"Mart's lawyer did that."

"Just the same, it looked mighty suspicious. You want to try the alley behind the tent?"

"Where does it lead?"

"Cuts back into the Via, at White Rose Park."

Anna started. "White rose?"

"We were there that first night," said Jacques. "You remember it—big rose-walled cul-de-sac. Fountain. Pretty, but not for us, not now. Has only one entrance. We'll have to try something else."

The psychiatrist said hesitantly: "No, wait."

For some moments she had been struck by the sinister contrast in this second descent into the Via and the irresponsible gaiety of that first night. The street, the booths, the laughter seemed the same, but really weren't. It was like a familiar musical score, subtly altered by some demoniac hand, raised into some harsh and fatalistic minor key. It was like the second movement of Tchaikovsky's *Romeo and Juliet*: all the bright promises of the first movement were here, but repetition had transfigured them into frightful premonitions.

She shivered. That second movement, that echo of destiny, was sweeping through her in ever faster tempo, as though impatient to consummate its assignation with her. Come safety, come death, she must yield to the pattern of repetition.

Her voice had a dream-like quality: "Take me again to the White Rose Park."

"What! Talk sense! Out here in the open you may have a chance."

"But I *must* go there. Please, Ruy. I think it's something about a white rose. Don't look at me as though I were crazy. Of course I'm crazy. If you don't want to take me, I'll go alone. But I'm going."

His hard eyes studied her in speculative silence, then he looked away. As the stillness grew, his face mirrored his deepening introspection. "At that, the possibilities are intriguing. Martha's stooges are sure to look in on you. But will they be able to see you? Is the hand that wields the pistol equally skilled with the brush and palette? Unlikely. Art and Science again. Pointillist school versus police school. A good one on Martha—if it works. Anna's dress is green. Complement of green is purple. Violet's dress should do it."

"My dress?" cried the old woman. "What are you up to, Ruy?"

"Nothing. Luscious. I just want you to take off one of your dresses. The outer one will do."

"Sir!" Violet began to sputter in barely audible gasps.

Anna had watched all this in vague detachment, accepting it as one of the man's daily insanities. She had no idea what he wanted with a dirty old purple dress, but she thought she knew how she could get it for him, while simultaneously introducing another repetitive theme into this second movement of her hypothetical symphony.

She said: "He's willing to make you a fair trade, Violet."

The spluttering stopped. The old woman eyed them both suspiciously. "Meaning what?"

"He'll drink one of your love potions."

The leathery lips parted in amazement. *"I'm* agreeable, if *he* is, but I know he isn't. Why, that scamp doesn't love any creature in the whole world, except maybe himself."

"And yet he's ready to make a pledge to his beloved," said Anna.

The artist squirmed. "I like you, Anna, but I won't be trapped. Anyway, it's all nonsense. What's a glass of acidified water between friends?"

"The pledge isn't to me, Ruy. It's to a Red Rose."

He peered at her curiously. "Oh? Well, if it will please you . . . All right, Violet, but off with that dress before you pour up."

Why, wondered Anna, do I keep thinking his declaration of love to a red rose is my death sentence? It's moving too fast. Who, what—is The Red Rose? The Nightingale dies in making the white rose red. So *she* —or I—can't be The Red Rose. Anyway, the Nightingale is ugly, and the Rose is beautiful. And why must The Student have a Red Rose? How will it admit him to his mysterious dance?

"Ah, Madame De Medici is back." Jacques took the glass and purple bundle the old woman put on the table. "What are the proper words?" he asked Anna.

"Whatever you want to say."

His eyes, suddenly grave, looked into hers. He said quietly: "If ever The Red Rose presents herself to me, I shall love her forever."

Anna trembled as he upended the glass.

CHAPTER SIXTEEN

A LITTLE later they slipped into the Park of the White Roses. The buds were just beginning to open, and thousands of white floreate eyes blinked at them in the harsh artificial light. As before, the enclosure was empty, and silent, save for the chattering splashing of its single fountain.

Anna abandoned a disconnected attempt to analyze the urge that had brought her here a second time. It's all too fatalistic, she thought, too involved. If I've entrapped myself, I can't feel bitter about it. "Just think," she murmured aloud, "in less than ten minutes it will all be over, one way or the other."

"Really? But where's my red rose?"

How could she even *consider* loving this jeering beast? She said coldly: "I think you'd better go. It may be rather messy in here soon." She thought of how her body would look, sprawling, misshapen, uglier than ever. She couldn't let him see her that way.

"Oh, we've plenty of time. No red rose, eh? Hmm. It seems to me, Anna, that you're composing yourself for death prematurely. There really is that little matter of the rose to be taken care of first, you know. As The Student, I must insist on my rights."

What made him be this way? "Ruy, please . . ." Her voice was trembling, and she was suddenly very near to tears.

"There, dear, don't apologize. Even the best of us are thoughtless at times. Though I must admit, I never expected such lack of consideration, such poor manners, in *you*. But then, at heart, you aren't really an artist. You've no appreciation of form." He began to untie the bundled purple dress, and his voice took on the argumentative dogmatism of a platform lecturer. "The perfection of form, of technique, is the highest achievement possible to the artist. When he subordinates form to subject matter, he degenerates eventually into a boot-lick, a scientist, or, worst of all, a Man with a Message. Here, catch!" He tossed the gaudy garment at Anna, who accepted it in rebellious wonder.

Critically, the artist eyed the nauseating contrast of the purple and green dresses, glanced momentarily toward the semi-circle of white-budded wall beyond, and then continued: "There's nothing like a school-within-a-school to squeeze dry the dregs of form. And whatever their faults, the pointillists of the impressionist movement could depict color with magnificent depth of chroma. Their palettes held only the spectral colors, and they never mixed them. Do you know why the Seines of Seurat are so brilliant and luminous? It's because the water is made of dots of pure green, blue, red and yellow, alternating with white in the proper proportion." He motioned with his hand, and she followed as he walked slowly on around the semi-circular gravel path. "What a pity Martha isn't here to observe our little experiment in tricolor stimulus. Yes, the scientific psychologists finally gave arithmetical vent to what the pointillists knew long before them—that a mass of points of any three spectral colors—or of one color and its complementary color—can be made to give any imaginable hue simply by varying their relative proportion."

Anna thought back to that first night of the street dancers. So *that* was why his green and purple polka dot academic gown had first seemed white!

At his gesture, she stopped and stood with her humped back barely touching the mass of scented buds. The arched entrance was a scant hundred yards to her right. Out in the Via an ominous silence seemed to be gathering. The Security men were probably roping off the area, certain of their quarry. In a minute or two, perhaps sooner, they would be at the archway, guns drawn.

She inhaled deeply and wet her lips.

The man smiled. "You hope I know what I'm doing, don't you? So do I."

"I think I understand your theory," said Anna, "but I don't think it has much chance of working."

"Tush, child." He studied the vigorous play of the fountain speculatively. "The pigment should never harangue the artist. You're forgetting that there isn't really such a color as white. The pointillists knew how to simulate white with alternating dots of primary colors long before the scientists learned to spin the same colors on a disc. And those old masters could even make white from just two colors: a primary and its complementary color. Your green dress is our primary; Violet's purple dress is its complementary. Funny, mix 'em as pigments into a homogeneous mass, and you get brown. But daub 'em on the canvas side by side, stand back the right distance, and they blend into white. All you have to do is hold Vi's dress at arm's length, at your side, with a strip of rosebuds and green leaves looking out between, and you'll have that white rose you came here in search of."

She demurred: "But the angle of visual interruption won't be small enough to blend the colors into white, even if the police don't come any nearer than the archway. The eye sees two objects as one only when the visual angle between the two is less than sixty seconds of arc."

"That old canard doesn't apply too strictly to colors. The artist relies more on the suggestibility of the mind rather than on the mechanical limitations of the retina. Admittedly, if our lean-jawed friends stared in your direction for more than a fraction of a second, they'd see you not as a whitish blur, but as a woman in green holding out a mass of something purple. But they aren't going to give your section of the park more than a passing glance." He pointed past the fountain toward the opposite horn of the semi-circular path. "I'm going to stand over *there,* and the instant someone sticks his head in through the archway, I'm going to start walking. Now, as every artist knows, normal people in western cultures absorb pictures from left to right, because they're laevo-dextro readers. So our agent's first glance will be toward you, and then his attention will be momentarily distracted by the fountain in the centre. And before he can get back to you, I'll start walking, and his eyes will have to come on to me. His attentive transition, of course, must be sweeping and imperative, yet so smooth, so subtle, that he will suspect no control. Something like Alexander's painting, *Lady on a Couch,* where the converging stripes of the lady's robe carry the eye forcibly from the lower left margin to her face at the upper right."

Anna glanced nervously toward the garden entrance, then whispered entreatingly. "Then you'd better go. You've got to be beyond the fountain when they look in."

He sniffed. "All right, I know when I'm not wanted. That's the gratitude I get for making you into a rose."

"I don't care a tinker's damn for a *white* rose. Scat!"

He laughed, then turned and started on around the path.

As Anna followed the graceful stride of his long legs, her face began to writhe in alternate bitterness and admiration. She groaned softly. "You—*fiend!* You gorgeous, egotistical, insufferable, unattainable *FIEND!* You aren't elated because you're saving my life; *I* am just a blotch of pigment in your latest masterpiece. *I hate you!*"

He was past the fountain now, and nearing the position he had earlier indicated.

She could see that he was looking toward the archway. She was afraid to look there.

Now he must stop and wait for his audience.

Only he didn't. His steps actually hastened.

That meant . . .

The woman trembled, closed her eyes, and froze into a paralytic stupor through which the crunch of the man's sandals filtered as from a great distance, muffled, mocking.

And then, from the direction of the archway, came the quiet scraping of more footsteps.

In the next split second she would know life or death.

But even now, even as she was sounding the iciest depths of her terror, her lips were moving with the clear insight of imminent death. "No, I don't hate you. I love you, Ruy. I have loved you from the first."

At that instant a blue-hot ball of pain began crawling slowly up within her body, along her spine, and then outward between her shoulder blades, into her spinal hump. The intensity of that pain forced her slowly to her knees and pulled her head back in an invitation to scream.

But no sound came from her convulsing throat.

It was unendurable, and she was fainting.

The sound of footsteps died away down the Via. At least Ruy's ruse had worked.

And as the mounting anguish spread over her back, she understood that all sound had vanished with those retreating footsteps, forever, because she could no longer hear, nor use her vocal chords. She had forgotten how, but she didn't care.

For her hump had split open, and something had flopped clumsily out of it, and she was drifting gently outward into blackness.

CHAPTER NINETEEN

THE glum face of Ruy Jacques peered out through the studio window into the night-awakening Via.

Before I met you, he brooded, loneliness was a magic, ecstatic blade drawn across my heart strings; it healed the severed strands with every beat, and I had all that I wanted save what I had to have—the Red Rose. My search for that Rose alone matters! I must believe this. I must not swerve, even for the memory of you, Anna, the first of my own kind I have ever met. I must not wonder if they killed you, nor even care. They must have killed you . . . It's been three weeks.

Now I can seek the Rose again. Onward into loneliness.

He sensed the nearness of familiar metal behind him. "Hello, Martha," he said, without turning. "Just get here?"

"Yes. How's the party going?" Her voice seemed carefully expressionless.

"Fair. You'll know more when you get the liquor bill."

"Your ballet opens tonight, doesn't it?" Still that studied tonelessness.

"You know damn well it doesn't." His voice held no rancour. "La Tanid took your bribe and left for Mexico. It's just as well. I can't abide a prima ballerina who'd rather eat than dance." He frowned slightly. Every bit of metal on the woman was singing in secret elation. She was thinking of a great triumph—something far beyond her petty victory in wrecking his opening night. His searching mind caught hints of something intricate, but integrated, completed—and deadly. Nineteen equations. The Jacques Rosette. Sciomnia.

"So you've finished your toy," he murmured. "You've got what you wanted, and you think you've destroyed what I wanted."

Her reply was harsh, suspicious. "How did you know, when not even Grade is sure? Yes, my weapon is finished. I can hold in one hand a thing that can obliterate your whole Via in an instant. A city, even a continent would take but a little longer. Science versus Art! Bah! This concrete embodiment of biophysics is the answer to your puerile Renaissance—your precious feather-bed world of music and painting! You and your kind are helpless when I and my kind choose to act. In the final analysis Science means *force*—the ability to control the minds and bodies of men."

The shimmering surface of his mind was now catching the faintest wisps of strange, extraneous impressions, vague and disturbing, and which did not seem to originate from metal within the room. In fact, he could not be sure they originated from metal at all.

He turned to face her. "How can Science control all men when it can't even control individuals—Anna van Tuyl, for example?"

She shrugged her shoulders. "You're only partly right. They failed to find her, but her escape was pure accident. In any event, she no longer represents any danger to me or to the political group that I control. Security has actually dropped her from their shoot-on-sight docket."

He cocked his head slightly and seemed to listen. "*You* haven't, I gather."

"You flatter her. She was never more than a pawn in our little game of Science versus Art. Now that she's off the board, and I've announced checkmate against you, I can't see that she matters."

"So Science announces checkmate? Isn't that a bit premature? Suppose Anna shows up again, with or without the conclusion of her ballet score? Suppose we find another prima? What's to keep us from holding *The Nightingale and the Rose* tonight, as scheduled?"

"Nothing," replied Martha Jacques coolly. "Nothing at all, except that Anna van Tuyl has probably joined your former prima at the South Pole by this time, and anyway, a new ballerina couldn't learn the score in the space of two hours, even if you found one. If this wishful thinking comforts you, why, pile it on!"

Very slowly Jacques put his wine glass on the nearby table. He washed his mind clear with a shake of his satyrish head, and strained every sense into receptivity. Something was being etched against that slurred background of laughter and clinking glassware. Then he sensed—or heard—something that brought tiny beads of sweat to his forehead and made him tremble.

"What's the matter with you?" demanded the woman.

As quickly as it had come, the chill was gone.

Without replying, he strode quickly into the centre of the studio.

"Fellow revellers!" he cried. "Let us prepare to double, nay, *re*-double our merriment!" With sardonic satisfaction he watched the troubled silence spread away from him, faster and faster, like ripples around a plague spot.

When the stillness was complete, he lowered his head,

stretched out his hand as if in horrible warning, and spoke in the tense spectral whisper of Poe's Roderick Usher:

"*Madmen! I tell you that she now stands without the door!*"

Heads turned; eyes bulged toward the entrance.

There, the door knob was turning slowly.

The door swung in, and left a cloaked figure framed in the doorway.

The artist started. He had been certain that this must be Anna.

It *must* be Anna, yet it could not be. The once frail, cruelly bent body now stood superbly erect beneath the shelter of the cloak. There was no hint of spinal deformity in this woman, and there were no marring lines of pain about her faintly smiling mouth and eyes, which were fixed on his. In one graceful motion her hands reached up beneath the cloak and set it back on her shoulders. Then, after an almost instantaneous *demi-plie,* she floated twice, like some fragile flower dancing in a summer breeze, and stood before him *sur les pointes,* with her cape billowing and fluttering behind her in mute encore.

Jacques looked down into eyes that were dark fires. But her continued silence was beginning to disturb and irritate him. He responded to it almost by reflex, refusing to admit to himself his sudden enormous happiness: "A woman without a tongue! By the gods! Her sting is drawn!" He shook her by the shoulders, roughly, as though to punish this fault in her that had drawn the familiar acid to his mouth.

Her arms moved up, cross-fashioned, and her hands covered his. She smiled, and a harp-arpeggio seemed to wing across his mind, and the tones rearranged themselves into words, like images on water suddenly smooth:

"Hello again, darling. Thanks for being glad to see me."

Something in him collapsed. His arms dropped and he turned his head away. "It's no good, Anna. Why'd you come back? Everything's falling apart. Even our ballet. Martha bought out our prima."

Again that lilting cascade of tones in his brain: "I know dear, but it doesn't matter. I'll sub beautifully for La Tanid. I know the part perfectly. And I know the Nightingale's death song, too."

"Hah!" he laughed harshly, annoyed at his exhibition of

discouragement and her ready sympathy. He stretched his right leg into a mocking *pointe tendue*. "Marvellous! You have the exact amount of drab clumsiness that we need in a Nightingale. And as for the death song, why of course you and you alone know how that ugly little bird feels when"—his eyes were fixed on her mouth in sudden, startled suspicion, and he finished the rest of the sentence inattentively, with no real awareness of its meaning—"when she dies on the thorn."

As he waited, the melody formed, vanished, and re-formed and resolved into the strangest thing he had ever known: "What you are thinking is true. My lips do not move. I cannot talk. I've forgotten how, just as we both forgot how to read and write. But even the plainest nightingale can sing, and make the white rose red."

This was Anna transfigured. Three weeks ago he had turned his back and left a diffident disciple to an uncertain fate. Confronting him now was this dark angel bearing on her face the luminous stamp of death. In some manner that he might never learn, the gods had touched her heart and body, and she had borne them straightway to him.

He stood, musing in alternate wonder and scorn. The old urge to jeer at her suddenly rose in his gorge. His lips contorted, then gradually relaxed, as an indescribable elation began to grow within him.

He could thwart Martha yet!

He leaped to the table and shouted: "Your attention, friends! In case you didn't get all this, we've found a ballerina! The curtain rises tonight on our première performance, as scheduled!"

Over the clapping and cheering, Dorran, the orchestra conductor, shouted: "Did I understand that Dr. van Tuyl has finished the Nightingale's death song? We'll have to omit that tonight, won't we? No chance to rehearse . . ."

Jacques looked down at Anna for a moment. His eyes were very thoughtful when he replied: "She says it won't be omitted. What I mean is, keep that thirty-eight rest sequence in the death scene. Yes, do that, and we shall see . . . what we shall see . . ."

"Thirty-eight rests as presently scored, then?"

"Yes. All right, boys and girls. Let's be on our way. Anna and I will follow shortly."

CHAPTER TWENTY

NOW it was a mild evening in late June, in the time of the full blooming of the roses, and the Via floated in a heady, irresistible tide of attar. It got into the tongues of the children and lifted their laughter and shouts an octave. It stained the palettes of the artists along the sidewalks, so that, despite the bluish glare of the artificial lights, they could paint only in delicate crimsons, pinks, yellows and whites. The petalled current swirled through the sideshows and eternally new exhibits and gave them a veneer of perfection; it eddied through the canvas flap of the vendress of love philters and erased twenty years from her face. It brushed a scented message across the responsive mouths of innumerable pairs of lovers, blinding them to the appreciative gaze of those who stopped to watch them.

And the lovely dead petals kept fluttering through the introspective mind of Ruy Jacques, clutching and whispering. He brushed their skittering dance aside and considered the situation with growing apprehension. In her recurrent Dreams he thought, Anna had always awakened just as the Nightingale began her death song. But now she knew the death song. So she knew the Dream's end. Well, it must not be so bad, or she wouldn't have returned. Nothing was going to happen, not really. He shot the question at her: There was no danger any more, was there? Surely the ballet would be a superb success? She'd be enrolled with the immortals.

Her reply was grave, yet it seemed to amuse her. It gave him a little trouble; there were no words for its exact meaning. It was something like "Immortality begins with death."

He glanced at her face uneasily. "Are you looking for trouble?"

"Everything will go smoothly."

After all, he thought, she believes she has looked into the future and has seen what will happen.

"The Nightingale will not fail The Student," she added with a queer smile. "You'll get your Red Rose."

"You can be plainer than that," he muttered. "Secrets . . . secrets . . . why all this you're-too-young-to-know business?"

But she laughed in his mind, and the enchantment of that laughter took his breath away. Finally he said: "I admit I don't know what you're talking about. But if you're about to get involved in anything on my account, forget it. I won't have it."

"Each does the thing that makes him happy. The Student will never be happy until he finds the Rose that will admit him to his Dance. The Nightingale will never be happy until the Student holds her in his arms and thinks her as lovely as a Red Rose. I think we may both get what we want."

He growled: "You haven't the faintest idea what you're talking about."

"Yes I have, especially right now. For ten years I've urged people not to inhibit their healthy inclinations. At the moment I don't have any inhibitions at all. It's a wonderful feeling. I've never been so happy, I think. For the first and last time in my life, I'm going to kiss you."

Her hand tugged at his sleeve. As he looked down into that enchanted face, he knew that this night was hers, that she was privileged in all things, and that whatever she willed must yield to her.

They had stopped at the temporarily-erected stagedoor. She rose *sur les pointes,* took his face in her palms, and like a hummingbird drinking her first nectar, kissed him on the mouth.

A moment later she led him into the dressing-room corridor.

He stifled a confused impulse to wipe the back of his hand across his lips. "Well . . . well, just remember to take it easy. Don't try to be spectacular. The artificial wings won't take it. Canvas stretched on duralite and piano wire calls for adagio. A fast pirouette, and they're ripped off. Besides, you're out of practice. Control your enthusiasm in Act I or you'll collapse in Act II. Now, run on to your dressing room. Cue in five minutes!"

CHAPTER TWENTY-ONE

THERE is a faint, yet distinct anatomical difference in the foot of the man and that of the woman, which keeps him earthbound, while permitting her, after long and arduous training, to soar *sur les pointes*. Owing to the great and varied beauty of the arabesques open to the ballerina poised on her extended toes, the male danseur at one time existed solely as a shadowy *porteur*, and was needed only to supply unobtrusive support and assistance in the exquisite *enchainements* of the ballerina. Iron muscles in leg and torso are vital in the danseur, who must help maintain the illusion that his whirling partner is made of fairy gossamer, seeking to wing skyward from his restraining arms.

All this flashed through the incredulous mind of Ruy Jacques as he whirled in a double *fouette* and followed from the corner of his eye the grey figure of Anna van Tuyl, as, wings and arms aflutter, she pirouetted in the second *enchainement* of Act I, away from him and toward the *maître de ballet*.

It was all well enough to give the illusion of flying, of alighting apparently weightless, in his arms—that was what the audience loved. But that it could ever *really* happen—*that* was simply impossible. Stage wings—things of grey canvas and duralite frames—couldn't subtract a hundred pounds from one hundred and twenty.

And yet . . . it had seemed to him that she had actually flown.

He tried to pierce her mind—to extract the truth from the bits of metal about her. In a gust of fury he dug at the metal outline of those remarkable wings.

In the space of seconds his forehead was drenched in cold sweat, and his hands were trembling. Only the fall of the curtain on the first act saved him as he stumbled through his exit *entrechat*.

What had Matt Bell said? "To communicate in his new language of music, one may expect our man of the future to develop specialized membranous organs, which, of course, like the tongue, will have dual functional uses, possibly leading to the conquest of time as the tongue has conquered space."

Those wings were not wire and metal, but flesh and blood.

He was so absorbed in his ratiocination that he failed to become aware of an acutely unpleasant metal radiation behind him until it was almost upon him. It was an intricate conglomeration of matter, mostly metal, resting perhaps a dozen feet behind his back, showering the lethal presence of his wife.

He turned with nonchalant grace to face the first tangible spawn of the Sciomnia formula.

It was simply a black metal box with a few dials and buttons. The scientist held it lightly in her lap as she sat at the side of the table.

His eyes passed slowly from it to her face, and he knew that in a matter of minutes Anna van Tuyl—and all Via Rosa beyond her—would be soot floating in the night wind.

Martha Jacques' face was sublime with hate. "Sit down," she said quietly.

He felt the blood leaving his cheeks. Yet he grinned with a fair show of geniality as he dropped into the chair. "Certainly. I've got to kill time somehow until the end of Act I."

She pressed a button on the box surface.

His volition vanished. His muscles were locked, immobile. He could not breathe.

Just as he was convinced that she planned to suffocate him, her finger made another swift motion toward the box, and he sucked in a great gulp of air. His eyes could move a little, but his larnyx was still paralyzed.

Then the moments began to pass, endlessly, it seemed to him.

The table at which they sat was on the right wing of the stage. The woman sat facing into the stage, while his back was to it. She followed the preparations of the troupe for

Act II with moody, silent eyes, he with straining ears and metal-empathic sense.

Only when he heard the curtain sweeping across the street-stage to open the second act did the woman speak.

"She *is* beautiful. And so graceful with those piano-wire wings, just as if they were part of her. I don't wonder she's the first woman who ever really interested you. Not that you really *love* her. You'll never love anyone."

From the depths of his paralysis he studied the etched bitterness of the face across the table. His lips were parched, and his throat a desert.

She thrust a sheet of paper at him, and her lip curled. "Are you still looking for that rose? Search no further, my ignorant friend. There it is—Sciomnia, complete, with its nineteen sub-equations."

The lines of unreadable symbols dug like nineteen relentless harpoons ever deeper into his twisting, racing mind.

The woman's face grimaced in fleeting despair. "Your own wife solves Sciomnia and you condescend to keep her company until you go on again at the end of Act III. I wish I had a sense of humor. All I knew was to paralyze your spinal column. Oh, don't worry. It's purely temporary. I just didn't want you to warn her. And I know what torture it is for you not to be able to talk." She bent over and turned a knurled knob on the side of the black steel box. "There, at least you can whisper. You'll be completely free after the weapon fires."

His lips moved in a rapid slur. "Let us bargain, Martha. Don't kill her. I swear never to see her again."

She laughed, almost gaily.

He pressed on. "But you have all you really want. Total fame, total power, total knowledge, the body perfect. What can her death and the destruction of the Via give you?"

"Everything."

"Martha, for the sake of all humanity to come, don't do this thing! I know something about Anna van Tuyl that perhaps even Bell doesn't—something she has concealed very adroitly. That girl is the most precious creature on earth!"

"It's precisely because of that opinion—which I do not necessarily share—that I shall include her in my general destruction of the Via." Her mouth slashed at him: "Oh, but it's wonderful to see you squirm. For the first time in your miserable thirty years of life you really want something. You've got to crawl down from that ivory tower of indifference and actually plead with me, whom you've never even taken the trouble to despise. You and your damned art. Let's see it save her now!"

The man closed his eyes and breathed deeply. In one rapid, complex surmise, he visualized an *enchainement* of postures, a *pas de deux* to be played with his wife as an unwitting partner. Like a skilled chess player, he had analyzed various variations of her probable responses to his gambit, and he had every expectation of a successful climax. And therein lay his hesitation, for success meant his own death.

Yes, he could not eradicate the idea from his mind. Even at this moment he believed himself intrigued more by the novel, if macabre, possibilities inherent in the theme rather than its superficial altruism. While seeming to lead Martha through an artistic approach to the murder of Anna and the Via, he could, in a startling, off key climax, force her to kill him instead. It amused him enormously to think that afterward, she would try to reduce the little comedy to charts and graph paper in an effort to discover how she had been hypnotized.

It was the first time in his life that he had courted physical injury. The emotional sequence was new, a little heady. He could do it; he need only be careful about his timing.

After hurling her challenge at him, the woman had again turned morose eyes downstage, and was apparently absorbed in a grudging admiration of the second act. But that couldn't last long. The curtain on Act II would be her signal.

And there it was, followed by a muffled roar of applause. He must stall her through most of Act III, and then . . .

He said quickly: "We still have a couple of minutes before the last act begins, where the Nightingale dies on the thorn. There's no hurry. You ought to take time to do this thing properly. Even the best assassinations are not purely a matter of science. I'll wager you never read De Quincey's little essay on murder as a fine art. No? You see, you're a neophyte, and could do with a few tips from an old hand. You must keep in mind your objects: to destroy both the Via and Anna. But mere killing won't be enough. You've got to make *me* suffer too. Suppose you shoot Anna when she comes on at the beginning of Act III. Only fair. The difficulty is that Anna and the others will never know what hit them. You don't give them the opportunity to bow to you as their conqueror."

He regarded her animatedly. "You see, can't you, my dear, that some extraordinarily difficult problems in composition are involved?"

She glared at him, and seemed about to speak.

He continued hastily: "Not that I'm trying to dissuade you. You have the basic concept, and despite your lack of experience, I don't think you'll find the problem of technique insuperable. Your prelude was rather well done: freezing me *in situ,* as it were, to state your theme simply and without adornment, followed immediately by variations of dynamic and suggestive portent. The finale is already implicit; yet it is kept at a disciplined arm's length while the necessary structure is formed to support it and develop its stern message."

She listened intently to him, and her eyes were narrow. The expression on her face said: "Talk all you like. This time, you won't win."

Somewhere beyond the flimsy building-board stage wing he heard Dorran's musicians tuning up for Act III.

His dark features seemed to grow even more earnest, but his voice contained a perceptible burble. "So you've blocked in the introduction and the climax. A beginning and an end. The *real* problem comes now: how much, and what kind—of a middle? Most beginning murderesses would simply give up in frustrated bafflement. A few would shoot the moment Anna floats into the white rose garden. In my opinion, however, considering the wealth of material inherent in your composition, such abbreviation would be inexcusably primitive and garish—if not actually vulgar."

Martha Jacques blinked, as though trying to break through some indescribable spell that was being woven about her. Then she laughed shortly. "Go on. I wouldn't miss this for anything. Just when *should* I destroy the Via?"

The artist sighed. "You see? Your only concern is the *result*. You completely ignore the *manner* of its accomplishment. Really, Mart, I should think you'd show more insight into your first attempt at serious art. Now please don't misunderstand me, dear. I have the warmest regard for your spontaneity and enthusiasm: to be sure, they're quite indispensable when dealing with hackneyed themes, but headlong eagerness is not a substitute for method, or for art. We must search out and exploit subsidiary themes, intertwine them in subtle counterpoint with the major motifs. The most obvious minor theme is the ballet itself. That ballet is the loveliest thing I've ever seen or heard. Nevertheless, *you* can give it a power, a dimension, that even Anna wouldn't suspect possible, simply by blending it contrapuntally into your own work. It's all a matter of firing at the proper instant." He smiled engagingly. "I see that you're beginning to appreciate the potentialities of such unwitting collaboration."

The woman studied him through heavy-lidded eyes. She said slowly: "You *are* a great artist—and a loathesome beast."

He smiled still more amiably. "Kindly restrict your appraisals to your fields of competence. You haven't, as yet, sufficient background to evaluate me as an artist. But let us return to your composition. Thematically, it's rather pleasing. The form, pacing, and orchestration are irreproachable. It is adequate. And its very adequacy condemns it. One detects a certain amount of diffident imitation and over-attention to technique common to artists working in a new medium. The overcautious sparks of genius aren't setting us aflame. The artist isn't getting enough of his own personality into the work. And the remedy is as simple as the diagnosis: the artist must penetrate his work, wrap it around him, give it the distilled, unique essence of his heart and mind, so that it will blaze up and reveal his soul even through the veil of unidiomatic technique."

He listened a moment to the music outside. "As Anna wrote her musical score, a hiatus of thirty-eight rests precedes the moment the nightingale drops dying from the thorn. At the start of that silence, you could start to run off your nineteen sub-equations in your little tin box, audio-Fourier style. You might even route the equations into the loudspeaker system, if our gadget is capable of remote control."

For a long time she appraised him calculatingly. "I finally think I understand you. You hoped to unnerve me with your savage, over-accentuated satire, and make me change my mind. So you aren't a beast, and even though I see through you, you're even a greater artist than I at first imagined."

He watched as the woman made a number of adjustments on the control panel of the black box. When she looked up again, her lips were drawn into hard purple ridges.

She said: "But it would be too great a pity to let such art go to waste, especially when supplied by the author of 'Twinkle, twinkle, little star'. And you will indulge an amateur musician's vanity if I play my first Fourier composition *fortissimo*."

He answered her smile with a fleeting one of his own. "An artist should never apologize for self-admiration. But watch your cueing. Anna should be clasping the white rose thorn to her breast in thirty seconds, and that will be your signal to fill in the first half of the thirty-eight rest hiatus. Can you see her?"

The woman did not answer, but he knew that her eyes were following the ballet on the invisible stage and Dorran's baton, beyond, with fevered intensity.

The music glided to a halt.

"Now!" hissed Jacques.

She flicked a switch on the box.

They listened, frozen, as the multi-throated public address system blared into life up and down the two miles of the Via Rosa.

The sound of Sciomnia was chill, metallic, like the cruel crackle of ice heard suddenly in the intimate warmth of an enchanted garden, and it seemed to chatter derisively, well aware of the magic that it shattered.

As it clattered and skirled up its harsh tonal staircase, it seemed to shriek: "Fools! Leave this childish nonsense and follow me! I am Science! I AM ALL!"

And, Ruy Jacques, watching the face of the prophetess of the God of Knowledge, was for the first time in his life aware of the possibility of utter defeat.

As he stared in mounting horror, her eyes rolled slightly

upward, as though buoyed by some irresistible inner flame, which the pale translucent cheeks let through.

But as suddenly as they had come, the nineteen chords were over, and then, as though to accentuate the finality of that mocking manifesto, a ghastly aural afterimage of silence began building up around his world.

For a near eternity it seemed to him that he and this woman were alone in the world, that, like some wicked witch, she had, through her cacophonic creation, immutably frozen the thousands of invisible watchers beyond the thin walls of the stage wings.

It was a strange, yet simple thing that broke the appalling silence and restored sanity, confidence, and the will to resist to the man: from somewhere far away, a child whimpered.

Breathing as deeply as his near paralysis would permit, the artist murmured: "Now, Martha, in a moment I think you will hear why I suggested your Fourier broadcast. I fear Science has been had once mo——"

He never finished, and her eyes, which were crystallising into question marks, never fired their barbs.

A towering tidal wave of tone was engulfing the Via, apparently of no human source and from no human instrument.

Even he, who had suspected in some small degree what was coming, now found his paralysis once more complete. Like the woman scientist opposite him, he could only sit in motionless awe, with eyes glazing, jaw dropping, and tongue cleaving to the roof of his mouth.

He knew that the heart strings of Anna van Tuyl were one with this mighty sea of song, and that it took its ecstatic timbre from the reverberating volutes of that godlike mind.

And as the magnificent chords poured out in exquisite consonantal sequence, now with a sudden reedy delicacy, now with the radiant gladness of cymbals, he knew that his plan must succeed.

For, chord for chord, tone for tone, and measure for measure, the Nightingale was repeating in her death song the nineteen chords of Martha Jacques' Sciomnia equations.

Only now those chords were transfigured, as though some Parnassian composer were compassionately correcting and magically transmuting the work of a dull pupil.

The melody spiralled heavenward on wings. It demanded no allegiance; it hurled no pronunciamento. It held a message, but one almost too glorious to be grasped. It was steeped in boundless aspiration, but it was at peace with man and his universe. It sparkled humility, and in its abnegation there was grandeur. Its very incompleteness served to hint at its boundlessness.

And then it, too, was over. The death song was done.

Yes, thought Ruy Jacques, it is the Sciomnia, rewritten, recast, and breathed through the blazing soul of a goddess. And when Martha realizes this, when she sees how I tricked her into broadcasting her trifling, inconsequential effort, she is going to fire her weapon—at *me*.

He watched the woman's face go livid, her mouth work in speechless hate.

"You *knew!*" she screamed. "You did it to humiliate me!"

Jacques began to laugh. It was a nearly silent laughter, rhythmic with mounting ridicule, pitiless in its mockery.

"Stop that!"

But his abdomen was convulsing in rigid helplessness, and tears began to stream down his cheeks.

"I warned you once before!" yelled the woman. Her hand darted toward the black box and turned its long axis toward the man.

Like a period punctuating the rambling, aimless sentence of his life, a ball of blue light burst from a cylindrical hole in the side of the box.

His laughter stopped suddenly. He looked from the box to the woman with growing amazement. He could bend his neck. His paralysis was gone.

She stared back, equally startled. She gasped: "Something went wrong! *You should be dead!*"

The artist didn't linger to argue.

In his mind was the increasingly urgent call of Anna van Tuyl.

CHAPTER TWENTY-TWO

DORRAN waved back the awed mass of spectators as Jacques knelt and transferred the faerie body from Bell's arms into his own.

"I'll carry you to your dressing room," he whispered. "I might have known you'd over-exert yourself."

Her eyes opened in the general direction of his face; in his mind came the tinkling of bells: "No . . . don't move me."

He looked up at Bell. "I think she's hurt! Take a look here!" He ran his hands over the seething surface of the wing folded along her side and breast: It was fevered fire.

"I can do nothing," replied the latter in a low voice. "She will tell you that I can do nothing."

"Anna!" cried Jacques. "What's wrong? What happened?"

Her musical reply formed in his mind. "Happened? Sciomnia was quite a thorn. Too much energy for one mind to disperse. Need two . . . three. Three could dematerialize weapon itself. Use wave formula of matter. Tell the others."

"*Others?* What are you talking about?" His thoughts whirled incoherently.

"Others like us. Coming soon. Bakine, dancing in streets of Leningrad. In Mexico City . . . the poetess Orteza. Many . . . this generation. *The Golden People*. Matt Bell guessed. Look!"

An image took fleeting form in his mind. First it was music, and then it was pure thought, and then it was a crisp strange air in his throat and the twang of something marvellous in his mouth. Then it was gone. "What was that?" he gasped.

"The Zhak symposium, seated at wine one April evening in the year 2437. Probability world. May . . . not occur. Did you recognize yourself?"

"Twenty-four thirty-seven?" His mind was fumbling.

"Yes. Couldn't you differentiate your individual mental contour from the whole? I thought you might. The group was still somewhat immature in the twenty-hundreds. By the fourteenth millennium . . ."

His head reeled under the impact of something titanic.

". . . your associated mental mass . . . creating a star of the M spectral class . . . galaxy now two-thirds terrestrialized . . ."

In his arms her wings stirred uneasily; all unconsciously he stroked the hot membranous surface and rubbed the marvellous bony framework with his fingers. "But Anna," he stammered, "I do not understand how this can be."

Her mind murmured in his. "Listen carefully, Ruy. Your pain . . . when your wings tried to open and couldn't . . . you needed certain psychoglandular stimulus. When you learn how to"—here a phrase he could not translate—"afterwards, they open . . ."

"When I learn—*what*?" he demanded. "What did you say I had to know, to open my wings?"

"One thing. The one thing . . . must have . . . to see the Rose."

"Rose—rose—*rose*!" he cried in near exasperation. "All right, then, my dutiful Nightingale, how long must I wait for you to make this remarkable Red Rose? I ask you, where is it?"

"Please . . . not just yet . . . in your arms just a little longer . . . while we finish ballet. Forget yourself, Ruy. Unless . . . leave prison . . . own heart . . . never find the Rose. Wings never unfold . . . remain a mortal. Science . . . isn't all. Art isn't . . . one thing greater . . . Ruy! I can't prolong . . ."

He looked up wildly at Bell.

The psychogeneticist turned his eyes away heavily. "Don't you understand? She has been dying ever since she absorbed that Sciomniac blast."

A faint murmur reached the artist's mind. "So you couldn't learn . . . poor Ruy . . . poor Nightingale . . ."

As he stared stuporously, her dun-colored wings began to shudder like leaves in an October wind.

From the depths of his shock he watched the fluttering of the wings give way to a sudden convulsive straining of her legs and thighs. It surged upward through her blanching body, through her abdomen and chest, pushing her blood before it and out into her wings, which now appeared more purple than grey.

To the old woman standing at his side, Bell observed quietly: "Even *homo superior* has his death struggle . . ."

The vendress of love philters nodded with anile sadness. "And she knew the answer . . . lost . . . lost . . ."

And still the blood came, making the wing membranes thick and taut.

"Anna!" shrieked Ruy Jacques. "You *can't* die. I won't let you! I love you! *I love you!*"

He had no expectation that she could still sense the images in his mind, nor even that she was still alive.

But suddenly, like stars shining their brief brilliance through a rift in storm clouds, her lips parted in a gay smile. Her eyes opened and seemed to bathe him in an intimate flow of light. It was during this momentary illumination, just before the lips solidified into their final enigmatic mask, that he thought he heard, as from a great distance, the opening measures of Weber's *Invitation to the Dance*.

At this moment the conviction formed in his numbed understanding that her loveliness was now supernal, that greater beauty could not be conceived or endured.

But even as he gazed in stricken wonder, the blood-gorged wings curled slowly up and out, enfolding the ivory breast and shoulders in blinding scarlet, like the petals of some magnificent rose.

THE CHESSPLAYERS

NOW please understand this. I'm not saying that all chessplayers are lunatics. But I do claim that chronic chessplaying affects a man.

Let me tell you about the K Street Chess Club, of which I was once treasurer.

Our membership roll claimed a senator, the leader of a large labor union, the president of the A. & W. Railroad, and a few other big shots. But it seemed the more important they were *outside,* the rottener they were as chessplayers.

The senator and the rail magnate didn't know the Ruy Lopez from the Queen's Gambit, so of course they could only play the other fish, or hang around wistfully watching the games of the Class A players and wishing that they, too, amounted to something.

The club's champion was Bobby Baker, a little boy in the fourth grade at the Pestalozzi-Borstal Boarding School. Several of his end game compositions had been published in *Chess Review* and *Shakhmatny Russkji Zhurnal* before he could talk plainly.

Our second best was Pete Summers, a clerk for the A. & W. Railroad. He was the author of two very famous chess books. One book proved that white can always win, and the other proved that black can always draw. As you might suspect, the gap separating him from the president of his railroad was abysmal indeed.

The show position was held by Jim Bradley, a chronic idler whose dues were paid by his wife. The club's admiration for him was profound.

But experts don't make a club. You have to have some guiding spirit, a fairly good player; with a knack for organization and a true knowledge of values.

Such a gem we had in our secretary, Nottingham Jones.

It was really my interest in Nottingham that led me to join the K Street Chess Club. I wanted to see if he was an exception, or whether they were all alike.

After I tell you about their encounter with Zeno, you can judge for yourself.

In his unreal life Nottingham Jones was a statistician in a government bureau. He worked at a desk in a big room with many other desks, including mine, and he performed his duties blankly and without conscious effort. Many an afternoon, after the quitting bell had rung and I had strolled over to discuss finances with him, he would be astonished to discover that he had already come to work and had turned out a creditable stack of forms.

I suppose that it was during these hours of his quasi-existence that the invisible Nottingham conceived those numerous events that had made him famous as a chess club emcee through the United States.

For it was Nottingham who organized the famous American-Soviet cable matches (in which the U.S. team had been so soundly trounced), refereed numerous U.S. match championships, and launched a dozen brilliant but impecunious foreign chess masters on exhibition tours in a hundred chess clubs from New York to Los Angeles.

But the achievements of which he was proudest were the bishop-knight tournaments.

Now the bishop is supposed to be slightly stronger than the knight, and this evaluation has become so ingrained in chess thinking today that no player will voluntarily exchange a bishop for an enemy knight. He may squander his life's savings on phony stock, talk back to traffic cops, and forget his wedding anniversary, but never, never, *never* will he exchange a bishop for a knight.

Nottingham suspected this fixation to be ill-founded; he had the idea that the knight was just as strong as the bishop, and to prove his point he held numerous intramural tournaments in the K Street Club, in which one player used six pawns and a bishop against the six pawns and a knight of his opponent.

Jones never did make up his mind as to whether the bishop was stronger than the knight, but at the end of a couple of years he did know that the K Street Club had more bishop-knight experts than any other club in the United States.

And it then occurred to him that American chess had a beautiful means of redeeming itself from its resounding defeat at the hands of the Russian cable team.

He sent his challenge to Stalin himself—the K Street Chess Club versus All the Russians—a dozen boards of bishop-knight games, to be played by cable.

The Soviet Recreation Bureau sent the customary six curt rejections and then promptly accepted.

And this leads us back to one afternoon at 5 o'clock when Nottingham Jones looked up from his desk and seemed startled to find me standing there.

"Don't get up yet," I said. "This is something you ought to take sitting down."

He stared at me owlishly. "Is the year's rent due again so soon?"

"Next week. This is something else."

"Oh?"

"A professor friend of mine," I said, "who lives in the garret over my apartment, wants to play the whole club at one sitting—a simultaneous exhibition."

"A simul, eh? Pretty good, is he?"

"It isn't exactly the professor who wants to play. It's really a friend of his."

"Is *he* good?"

"The professor says so. But that isn't exactly the point. To make it short, this professor, Dr. Schmidt, owns a pet rat. He wants the rat to play." I added: "And for the usual simul fee. The professor needs money. In fact, if he doesn't get a steady job pretty soon he may be deported."

Nottingham looked dubious. "I don't see how we can help him. Did you say *rat*?"

"I did."

"A chessplaying rat? A four-legged one?"

"Right. Quite a drawing card for the club, eh?"

Nottingham shrugged his shoulders. "We learn something every day. Will you believe it, I never heard they cared for the game. Women don't. However, I once read about an educated horse . . . I suppose he's well known in Europe?"

"Very likely," I said. "The professor specializes in comparative psychology."

Nottingham shook his head impatiently. "I don't mean the professor. I'm talking about the rat. What's his name, anyway."

"Zeno."

"Never heard of him. What's his tournament score?"

"I don't think he ever played in any tournaments. The professor taught him the game in a concentration camp. How good he is I don't know, except that he can give the professor rook odds."

Nottingham smiled pityingly. "I can give you rook odds, but I'm not good enough to throw a simul."

A great light burst over me. "Hey, wait a minute. You're completely overlooking the fantastic fact that Zeno is a—"

"The only pertinent question," interrupted Nottingham, "is whether he's really in the *master* class. We've got half a dozen players in the club who can throw an 'inside' simul for free, but when we hire an outsider and charge the members a dollar each to play him, he's got to be good enough to tackle *our* best. And when the whole club's in training for the bishop-knight cable match with the Russians next month, I can't have them relaxing over a mediocre simul."

"But you're missing the whole point—"

"—which is, this Zeno needs money and you want me to throw a simul to help him. But I just can't do it. I have a duty to the members to maintain a high standard."

"But Zeno is a rat. He learned to play chess in a concentration camp. He—"

"That doesn't necessarily make him a good player."

It was all cockeyed. My voice trailed off. "Well, somehow it seemed like a good idea."

Nottingham saw that he had let me down too hard. "If you want to, you might arrange a game between Zeno and one of our top players—say Jim Bradley. He has lots of time. If Jim says Zeno is good enough for a simul, we'll give him a simul."

So I invited Jim Bradley and the professor, including Zeno, to my apartment the next evening.

I had seen Zeno before, but that was when I thought he was just an ordinary pet rat. Viewed as a chessmaster he seemed to be a completely different creature. Both Jim and I studied him closely when the professor pulled him out of his coat pocket and placed him on the chess table.

You could tell, just by looking at the little animal, from the way his beady black eyes shone and the alert way he carried his head, that here was a super-rat, an Einstein among rodents.

"Chust let him get his bearings," said the professor, as he fixed a little piece of cheese to Bradley's king with a thumb tack. "And don't worry, he will make a good showing."

Zeno pitter-pattered around the board, sniffed with a bored delicacy at both his and Bradley's chess pieces, twitched his nose at Bradley's cheese-crowned king, and gave the impression that the only reason he didn't yawn was that he was too well bred. He returned to his side of the board and waited for Bradley to move.

Jim blinked, shook himself, and finally pushed his queen pawn two squares.

Zeno minced out, picked up his own queen pawn between his teeth, and moved it forward two squares. Then Jim moved out his queen bishop pawn, and the game was under way, a conventional Queen's Gambit Declined.

I got the professor off in a corner. "How did you teach him to play? You never did tell me."

"Was easy. Tied each chessman in succession to body and let Zeno run simple maze on the chessboard composed of moves of chess man, until reached king and got piece of bread stuck on crown. Next, ve—one moment, please."

We both looked at the board. Zeno had knocked over Jim's king and was tapping with his dainty forefoot in front of the fallen monarch.

Jim was counting the taps with silent lips. "He's announcing a mate in thirteen. And he's right."

Zeno was already nibbling at the little piece of cheese fixed to Jim's king.

When I reported the result to Nottingham the next day, he agreed to hold a simultaneous exhibition for Zeno. Since Zeno was an unknown, with no reputation and no drawing power, Jones naturally didn't notify the local papers, but merely sent post cards to the club members.

On the night of the simul Nottingham set up 25 chess tables in an approximate circle around the club room. Here and there the professor pushed the tables a little closer together so that Zeno could jump easily from one to the other as he made his rounds. Then the professor made a circuit of all the tables and tacked a little piece of cheese to each king.

After that he mopped at his face, stepped outside the circle, and Zeno started his rounds.

And then we hit a snag.

A slow grey man emerged from a little group of spectators and approached the professor.

"Dr. Hans Schmidt?" he asked.

"Ya," said the professor, a little nervously. "I mean, yes sir."

The grey man pulled out his pocketbook and flashed

something at the professor. "Immigration service. Do you have in your possession a renewed immigration visa?"

The professor wet his lips and shook his head wordlessly.

The other continued. "According to our records you don't have a job, haven't paid your rent for a month, and your credit has run out at the local delicatessen. I'm afraid I'll have to ask you to come along with me."

"You mean—*deportation*?"

"How do I know? Maybe, maybe not."

The professor looked as though a steam roller had just passed over him. "So it comes," he whispered. "I knew I should not haf come out from hiding, but one needs money. . . ."

"Too bad," said the immigration man. "Of course, if you could post a $500 bond as surety for your self-support—"

"Had I $500, would I be behind at the delicatessen?"

"No, I guess not. That your hat and coat?"

The professor started sadly toward the coat-racks.

I grabbed at his sleeve.

"Now hold on," I said hurriedly. "Look, mister, in two hours Dr. Schmidt will have a contract for a 52-week exhibition tour." I exclaimed to the professor: "Zeno will make you all the money you can spend! When the simul is over tonight, Nottingham Jones will recommend you to every chess club in the United States, Canada, and Mexico. Think of it! Zeno! History's only chess-playing rat!"

"Not so fast," said Nottingham, who had just walked up. "I've got to see how good this Zeno is before I back him."

"Don't worry," I said. "Why, the bare fact that he's a rat—"

The grey man interrupted. "You mean you want me to wait a couple of hours until we see whether the professor is going to get some sort of contract?"

"That's right," I said eagerly. "After Zeno shows what he can do, the professor gets a chess exhibition tour."

The grey man was studying Zeno with distant distaste. "Well, okay. I'll wait."

The professor heaved a gigantic sigh and trotted off to watch his protégé.

"Say," said the grey man to me, "you people ought to

keep a cat in this place. I was sure I saw a rat running around over there."

"That's Zeno," I said. "He's playing chess."

"Don't get sarcastic, Jack. I was just offering a suggestion." He wandered off to keep an eye on the professor.

The evening wore on, and the professor used up all his handkerchiefs and borrowed one of mine. But I couldn't see what he was worried about, because it was clear that Zeno was a marvel, right up there in the ranks of Lasker, Alekhine, and Botvinnik.

In every game, he entered into an orgy of complications. One by one his opponents teetered off the razor's edge, and had to resign. One by one the tables emptied, and the losers gathered around those who were still struggling. The clusters around Bobby Baker, Pete Summers, and Jim Bradley grew minute by minute.

But at the end of the second hour, when only the three club champions were still battling, I noticed that Zeno was slowing down.

"What's wrong, professor?" I whispered anxiously.

He groaned. "For supper he chenerally gets only two little pieces cheese."

And so far tonight Zeno had eaten twenty-three! He was so fat he could hardly waddle.

I groaned too, and thought of tiny stomach pumps.

We watched tensely as Zeno pulled himself slowly from Jim Bradley's board to Pete Summers'. It seemed to take him an extraordinarily long time to analyze the position on Pete's board. At last he made his move and crawled across to Bobby Baker's table.

And it was there, chin resting on the pedestal of his king rook, that he collapsed into gentle rodent slumber.

The professor let out an almost inaudible but heart-rending moan.

"Don't just stand there!" I cried. "Wake him up!"

The professor prodded the little animal gingerly with his forefinger. *"Liebchen,"* he pleaded, *"wach' auf!"*

But Zeno just rolled comfortably over on his back.

A deathly silence had fallen over the room, and it was on account of this that we heard what we heard.

Zeno began to snore.

Everybody seemed to be looking in other directions

when the professor lifted the little animal up and dropped him tenderly into his wrinkled coat pocket.

The grey man was the first to speak. "Well, Dr. Schmidt? No contract?"

"Don't be silly," I declared. "Of course he gets a tour. Nottingham, how soon can you get letters off to the other clubs?"

"But I really can't recommend him," demurred Nottingham. "After all, he defaulted three out of 25 games. He's only a *Kleinmeister*—not the kind of material to make a simul circuit."

"What if he *didn't* finish three measly games? He's a good player, all the same. All you have to do is say the word and every club secretary in North America will make a date with him—at an entrance fee of $5 per player. He'll take the country by storm!"

"I'm sorry," Nottingham said to the professor. "I have a certain standard, your boy just doesn't make the grade."

The professor sighed. "*Ja, ich versteh*'."

"But this is crazy!" My voice sounded a little louder than I had intended. "You fellows don't agree with Nottingham, do you? How about you, Jim?"

Jim Bradley shrugged his shoulders. "Hard to say just how good Zeno is. It would take a week of close analysis to say definitely who has the upper hand in *my* game. He's a pawn down, but he has a wonderful position."

"But Jim," I protested. "That isn't the point at all. Can't you see it? Think of the publicity . . . a chess-playing *rat* . . . !"

"I wouldn't know about his personal life," said Jim curtly.

"Fellows!" I said desperately. "Is this the way all of you feel? Can't enough of us stick together to pass a club resolution recommending Zeno for a simul circuit? How about you, Bobby?"

Bobby looked uncomfortable. "I think the school station wagon is waiting for me. I guess I ought to be getting back."

"Coming, doc?" asked the grey man.

"Yes," replied Dr. Schmidt heavily. "Good evening, chentlemen." I just stood there, stunned.

"Here's Zeno's income for the evening, professor," said Nottingham, pressing an envelope in his hand. "I'm afraid it won't help much, though, especially since I didn't feel justified in charging the customary dollar fee."

The professor nodded, and in numb silence I watched him accompany the immigration officer to the doorway.

The professor and I versus the chessplayers. We had thrown our Sunday punches, but we hadn't even scratched their gambit.

Just then Pete Summers called out. "Hey, Dr. Schmidt!" He held up a sheet of paper covered with chess diagrams. "This fell out of your pocket when you were standing here."

The professor said something apologetic to the grey man and came back. "*Danke*," he said, reaching for the paper. "Is part of a manuscript."

"A *chess* manuscript, professor?" I was grasping at straws now. "Are you writing a chess book?"

"Ya, I guess."

"Well, well," said Pete Summers, who was studying the sheet carefully. "The bishop against the knight, eh?"

"Ya. Now if you excuse me—"

"The bishop versus the knight?" shrilled Bobby Baker, who had trotted back to the tables.

"The bishop and knight?" muttered Nottingham Jones. He demanded abruptly: "Have you studied the problem long, professor?"

"Many months. In camp . . . in attic. And now manuscript has reached 2,000 pages, and we look for publisher."

"*We* . . . ?" My voice may have trembled a little, because both Nottingham and the professor turned and looked at me sharply. "Professor"—my words spilled out in a rush—"did Zeno write that book?"

"Who else?" answered the professor in wonder.

"I don't see how he could hold a pen," said Nottingham doubtfully.

"Not necessary," said the professor. "He made moves, and I wrote down." He added with wistful pride: "Zenchen is probably world's greatest living authority on bishop-knight."

The room was suddenly very still again. For an overlong moment the only sound was Zeno's muffled snoring spiraling up from the professor's pocket.

"Has he reached any conclusions?" breathed Nottingham.

The professor turned puzzled eyes to the intent faces about him. "Zeno believes conflict cannot be cheneralized. However, has discovered 78 positions in which bishop superior to knight and 24 positions in which knight is better. Obviously, player mit bishop must try—"

"—for one of the winning bishop positions, of course, and ditto for the knight," finished Nottingham. "That's an extremely valuable manuscript."

All this time I had been getting my first free breath of the evening. It felt good. "It's too bad," I said casually, "that the professor can't stay here long enough for you sharks to study Zeno's book and pick up some pointers for the great bishop-knight cable match next month. It's too bad, too, that Zeno won't be here to take a board against the Russians. He'd give us a sure point on the score."

"Yeah," said Jim Bradley. "He would."

Nottingham shot a question at the professor. "Would Zeno be willing to rent the manuscript to us for a month?"

The professor was about to agree when I interrupted. "That would be rather difficult, Nottingham. Zeno doesn't know where he'll be at the end of the month. Furthermore, as treasurer for the club, let me inform you that after we pay the annual rent next week, the treasury will be as flat as a pancake."

Nottingham's face fell.

"Of course," I continued carefully, "if you were willing to underwrite a tour for Zeno, I imagine he'd be willing to lend it to you for nothing. And then the professor wouldn't have to be deported, and Zeno could stay and coach our team, as well as take a board in the cable match."

Neither the professor or I breathed as we watched Nottingham struggling over that game of solitaire chess with his soul. But finally his owlish face gathered itself into an austere stubbornness. "I still can't recommend Zeno for a tour. I have my standards."

Several of the other players nodded gloomily.

"I'm scheduled to play against Kereslov," said Pete Summers, looking sadly at the sheet of manuscript. "But I agree with you, Nottingham."

I knew about Kereslov. The Moscow Club had been holding intramural bishop-knight tournaments every week for the past six months, and Kereslov had won nearly all of them.

"And I have to play Botvinnik," said Jim Bradley. He added feebly, "but you're right, Nottingham. We can't ethically underwrite a tour for Zeno."

Botvinnik was merely chess champion of the world.

"What a shame," I said. "Professor, I'm afraid we'll have to make a deal with the Soviet Recreation Bureau." It was just a sudden screwy inspiration. I still wonder whether I would have gone through with it if Nottingham hadn't said what he said next.

"Mister," he asked the immigration official, "you want $500 put up for Dr. Schmidt?"

"That's the customary bond."

Nottingham beamed at me. "We have more than that in the treasury, haven't we?"

"Sure. We have exactly $500.14, of which $500 is for rent. Don't look at me like that."

"The directors of this club," declared Nottingham sonorously, "hereby authorize you to draw a check for $500 payable to Dr. Schmidt."

"Are you cuckoo?" I yelped. "Where do you think I'm going to get another $500 for the rent? You lunatics will wind up playing your cable match in the middle of K Street!"

"This," said Nottingham coldly, "is the greatest work on chess since Murray's *History*. After we're through with it, I'm sure we can find a publisher for Zeno. Would you stand in the way of such a magnificent contribution to chess literature?"

Pete Summers chimed in accusingly. "Even if you can't be a friend to Zeno, you could at least think about the good of the club and of American chess. You're taking a very funny attitude about this."

"But of course you aren't a real chessplayer," said Bobby Baker sympathetically. "We never had a treasurer who was."

Nottingham sighed. "I guess it's about time to elect another treasurer."

"All right," I said bleakly. "I'm just wondering what I'm going to tell the landlord next week. He isn't a chessplayer either." I told the grey man, "Come over here to the desk, and I'll make out a cheque."

He frowned. "A cheque? From a bunch of chessplayers? Not on your life! Let's go, professor."

Just then a remarkable thing happened. One of our most minor members spoke up.

"I'm Senator Brown, one of Mr. Jones's *fellow chessplayers*. I'll endorse that cheque, if you like."

And then there was a popping noise and a button flew by my ear. I turned quickly to see a vast blast of smoke terminated by three perfect smoke rings. Our rail magnate tapped at his cigar. "I'm Johnson, of the A. & W. *We chessplayers* stick together on these matters. I'll endorse that cheque, too. And Nottingham, don't worry about the rent. The senator and I will take care of that."

I stifled an indignant gasp. *I* was the one worrying about the rent, not Nottingham. But of course I was beneath their notice. I wasn't a *chessplayer*.

The grey man shrugged his shoulders. "Okay, I'll take the bond and recommend an indefinite renewal."

Five minutes later I was standing outside the building gulping in the fresh cold air when the immigration officer walked past me toward his car.

"Goodnight," I said.

He ducked a little, then looked up. When he answered, he seemed to be talking more to himself than to me. "It was the funniest thing. You got the impression there was a little rat running around on those boards and moving the pieces with his teeth. But of course rats don't play chess. Just human beings." He peered at me through the dusk, as though trying to get things in focus. "There wasn't really a rat playing chess in there, was there?"

"No," I said. "There wasn't any rat in there. And no human beings, either. Just chessplayers."

THE NEW REALITY

CHAPTER ONE

PRENTISS crawled into the car, drew the extension connector of his concealed throat mike from its clip in his right sleeve, and plugged it into the ignition key socket.

In a moment he said curtly: "Get me the Censor."

The seconds passed as he heard the click of forming circuits. Then: "E speaking."

"Prentiss, honey."

"Call me 'E' Prentiss. What news?"

"I've met five classes under Professor Luce. He has a private lab. Doesn't confide in his graduate students. Evidently conducting secret experiments in comparative psychology. Rats and such. Nothing overtly censorable."

"I see. What are your plans?"

"I'll have his lab searched tonight. If nothing turns up, I'll recommend a drop."

"I'd prefer that you search the lab yourself."

A. Prentiss Rogers concealed his surprise and annoyance. "Very well."

His ear button clicked a dismissal.

With puzzled irritation he snapped the plug from the dash socket, started the car, and eased it down the drive into the boulevard bordering the university.

Didn't she realize that he was a busy Field Director with a couple of hundred men under him fully capable of making a routine night search? Undoubtedly she knew just that, but nevertheless was requiring that he do it himself. Why?

And why had she assigned Professor Luce to him personally, squandering so many of his precious hours, when half a dozen of his bright young physical philosophers could have handled it? Nevertheless E, from behind the august anonymity of her solitary initial, had been adamant. He'd never been able to argue with such cool beauty, anyway.

A mile away he turned into a garage on a deserted side street and drew up alongside a Cadillac.

Crush sprang out of the big car and silently held the rear door open for him.

Prentiss got in. "We have a job tonight."

His aide hesitated a fraction of a second before slamming the door behind him. Prentiss knew that the squat, asthmatic little man was surprised and delighted.

As for Crush, he'd never got it through his head that the control of human knowledge was a grim and hateful business, not a kind of cruel lark.

"Very good, sir," wheezed Crush, climbing in behind the wheel. "Shall I reserve a sleeping room at the Bureau for the evening?"

"Can't afford to sleep," grumbled Prentiss. "Desk so high now I can't see over it. Take a nap yourself, if you want to."

"Yes, sir. If I feel the need of it, sir."

The ontologist shot a bitter glance at the back of the man's head. No, Crush wouldn't sleep, but not because worry would keep him awake. A holdover from the days when all a Censor man had was a sleepless curiosity and a pocket Geiger, Crush was serenely untroubled by the dangerous and unfathomable implications of philosophical nucleonics. For Crush, "ontology" was just another definition in the dictionary: "The science of reality."

The little aide could never grasp the idea that unless a sane world-wide pattern of nucleonic investigation were followed, someone in Australia—or next door—might one day throw a switch and alter the shape of that reality. That's what made Crush so valuable; he just didn't know enough to be afraid. . . .

Prentiss had clipped the hairs from his nostrils and so far had breathed in complete silence. But now, as that cavernous face was turned toward where he lay stomach-to-earth in the sheltering darkness, his lungs convulsed in an audible gasp.

The mild, polite, somewhat abstracted academic features of Professor Luce were transformed. The face beyond the lab window was now flushed with blood, the thin lips were drawn back in soundless demoniac amusement, the sunken black eyes were dancing with red pinpoints of flame.

By brute will the ontologist forced his attention back to the rat.

Four times in the past few minutes he had watched the animal run down an inclined chute until it reached a fork, choose one fork, receive what must be a nerve-shattering electrc shock, and then be replaced in the chute-beginning for the next run. No matter which alternative fork was chosen, the animal always had been shocked into convulsions.

On this fifth run the rat, despite needling blasts of compressed air from the chute walls, was slowing down. Just before it reached the fork it stopped completely.

The air jets struck at it again, and little cones of upended grey fur danced on its rump and flanks.

It gradually ceased to tremble; its respiration dropped to normal. It seemed to Prentiss that its eyes were shut.

The air jets lashed out again. It gave no notice, but just lay there, quiescent, in a near coma.

As he peered into the window, Prentiss saw the tall man walk languidly over to the little animal and run a long hooklike forefinger over its back. No reaction. The professor then said something, evidently in a soft slurred voice, for Prentiss had difficulty in reading his lips.

"—when both alternatives are wrong for you, but you *must* do something, you hesitate, don't you, little one? You slow down, and you are lost. You are no longer a rat. Do you know what the universe would be like if a *photon* should slow down? You don't? Have you ever taken a bite out of a balloon, little friend? Just the tiniest possible bite?"

Prentiss cursed. The professor had turned and was walking toward the cages with the animal, and although he was apparently still talking, his lips were no longer visible.

After re-latching the cage-door the professor walked toward the lab entrance, glanced carefully around the room, and then, as he was reaching for the light switch, looked toward Prentiss' window.

For a moment the investigator was convinced that by some nameless power the professor was looking into the darkness, straight into his eyes.

He exhaled slowly. It was preposterous.

The room was plunged in darkness.

The investigator blinked and closed his eyes. He wouldn't really have to worry until he heard the lab door opening on the opposite side of the little building.

The door didn't open. Prentiss squinted into the darkness of the room.

Where the professor's head had been were now two mysterious tiny red flames, like candles.

Something must be reflecting from the professor's corneas. But the room was dark; there was no light to be reflected. The flame-eyes continued their illusion of studying him.

The hair was crawling on the man's neck when the twin lights finally vanished and he heard the sound of the lab door opening.

As the slow heavy tread died away down the flagstones to the street, Prentiss gulped in a huge lungful of the chill night air and rubbed his sweating face against his sleeve.

What had got into him? He was acting like the greenest cub. He was glad that Crush had to man the televisor relay in the Cadillac and couldn't see him.

He got to his hands and knees and crept silently toward the darkened window. It was a simple sliding sash, and a few seconds sufficed to drill through the glass and insert a hook around the sash lock. The rats began a nervous squeaking as he lowered himself into the darkness of the basement room.

His ear-receptor sounded. "The prof is coming back!" wheezed Crush's tinny voice.

Prentiss said something under his breath, but did not pause in drawing his infra-red scanner from his pocket.

He touched his fingers to his throat-mike. "Signal when he reaches the bend in the walk," he hissed. "And be sure you get this on the visor tape."

The apparatus got his first attention.

The investigator had memorized its position perfectly. Approaching as closely in the darkness as he dared, he "panned" the scanner over some very interesting apparatus that he had noticed on the table.

Then he turned to the books on the desk, regretting that he wouldn't have time to record more than a few pages.

"He's at the bend," warned Crush.

"Okay," mumbled Prentiss, running sensitive fingers over the book bindings. He selected one, opened it at random, and ran the scanner over the invisible pages. "Is this coming through?" he demanded.

"Chief, *he's at the door!*"

Prentiss had to push back the volume without scanning any more of it. He had just relocked the sash when the lab door swung open.

CHAPTER TWO

A COUPLE of hours later the ontologist bid a cynical good-morning to his receptionist and secretaries and stepped into his private office. He dropped with tired thoughtfulness into his swivel chair and pulled out the infrared negatives that Crush had prepared in the Cadillac darkroom. The page from the old German diary was particularly intriguing. He laboriously translated it once more:

> As I got deeper into the manuscript, my mouth grew dry, and my heart began to pound. This, I knew, was a contribution the like of which my family has not seen since Copernicus, Roger Bacon, or perhaps even Aristotle. It seemed incredible that this silent little man, who had never been outside of Koenigsberg, should hold the key to the universe—the *Critique of Pure Reason,* he calls it. And I doubt that even he realizes the ultimate portent of his teaching, for he says we cannot know the real shape or nature of anything, that is, the Thing-in-Itself, the Ding-an-Sich, or *noumenon*. He holds that this is the ultimate unknowable, reserved to the gods. He doesn't suspect that, century by century, mankind is nearing this final realization of the final things. Even this brilliant man would probably say that the earth was round in 600 B.C., even as it is today. But *I* know it was flat, then—as truly flat as it is truly round today. What

has changed? Not the Thing-in-Itself we call the Earth. No, it is the mind of man that has changed. But in his preposterous blindness, he mistakes what is really his own mental quickening for a broadened application of science and more precise methods of investigation—

Prentiss smiled.

Luce was undoubtedly a collector of philosophic incunabula. Odd hobby, but that's all it could be—a hobby. Obviously the earth had never been flat, and in fact hadn't changed shape substantially in the last couple of billion years. Certainly any notions as to the flatness of the earth held by primitives of a few thousand years ago or even by contemporaries of Kant were due to their ignorance rather than to accurate observation, and a man of Luce's erudition could only be amused by them.

Again Prentiss found himself smiling with the tolerance of a man standing on the shoulders of twenty centuries of science. The primitives, of course, did the best they could. They just didn't know. They worked with childish premises and infantile instruments.

His brows creased. To assume they had used childish premises was begging the question. On the other hand, was it really worth a second thought? All he could hope to discover would be a few instances of how inferior apparatus coupled perhaps with unsophisticated deductions had oversimplified the world of the ancients. Still, anything that interested the strange Dr. Luce automatically interested him, Prentiss, until the case was closed.

He dictated into the scriptor:

"Memorandum to Geodetic Section. Rush a paragraph history of ideas concerning shape of earth. Prentiss."

Duty done, he promptly forgot it and turned to the heavy accumulation of reports on his desk.

A quarter of an hour later the scriptor rang and began typing an incoming message.

> To the Director. Re your request for brief history of earth's shape. Chaldeans and Babylonians (per clay tablets from library of Assurbanipal), Egyptians (per Ahmes papyrus, ca. 1700 B.C.), Cretans (per inscriptions in royal library at Knossos, ca. 1300 B.C.), Chinese (per Chou Kung ms. ca. 1100 B.C.), Phoeni-

cians (per fragments at Tyre ca. 900 B.C.), Hebrews (per unknown Biblical historian ca. 850 B.C.), and early Greeks per map of widely-traveled geographer Hecataeus, 517 B.C.) assumed earth to be flat disc. But from the 5th century B.C. forward earth's sphericity universally recognized. . . .

There were a few more lines, winding up with the work done on corrections for flattening at poles, but Prentiss had already lost interest. The report threw no light on Luce's hobby and was devoid of ontological implications.

He tossed the script into the waste basket and returned to the reports before him.

A few minutes later he twisted uneasily in his chair, eyed the scriptor in annoyance, then forced himself back to his work.

No use.

Deriding himself for an idiot, he growled at the machine:

"Memorandum to Geodetic. Re your memo history earth's shape. How do you account for change to belief in sphericity after Hecataeus? Rush. Prentiss."

The seconds ticked by.

He drummed on his desk impatiently, then got up and began pacing the floor.

When the scriptor rang, he bounded back and leaned over his desk, watching the words being typed out.

Late Greeks based spherical shape on observation that mast of approaching ship appeared first, then prow. Not known why similar observation not made by earlier seafaring peoples. . . .

Prentiss rubbed his cheek in perplexity. What was he fishing for?

He thrust the half-born conjecture that the earth really had once been flat back into his mental recesses.

Well, then how about the heavens? Surely there was no record of their having changed during man's brief lifetime.

He'd try one more shot and quit.

"Memo to Astronomy Division. Rush paragraph on early vs. modern sun size and distance."

A few minutes later he was reading the reply:

Skipping Plato, whose data are believed baseless (he measured sun's distance at only twice that of moon), we come to earliest recognized "authority." Ptolemy (Almagest, ca. 140 A.D.) measured sun radius as 5.5 that of earth (as against 109 actual) measured sun distance at 1210 (23,000 actual). Fairly accurate measurements date only from 17th and 18th centuries.

. . .

He'd read all that somewhere. The difference was easily explained by their primitive instruments. It was insane to keep this up.

But it was too late.

"Memo to Astronomy. Were erroneous Ptolemaic measurements due to lack of precision instruments?"

Soon he had his reply:

To Director: Source of Ptolemy's errors in solar measurement not clearly understood. Used astrolabe precise to 10 seconds and clepsydra water clock incorporating Hero's improvements. With same instruments, and using modern value of pi, Ptolemy measured moon radius (0.29 earth radius vs. 0.273 actual) and distance (59 earth radii vs. 60 1/3 actual). Hence instruments reasonably precise. And note that Copernicus, using quasi-modern instruments and technique, "confirmed" Ptolemaic figure of sun's distance at 1200 earth radii. No explanation known for glaring error.

Unless, suggested something within Prentiss' mind, the sun were closer and much different before the 17th century, when Newton was telling the world where and how big the sun *ought* to be. But *that* solution was too absurd for further consideration. He would sooner assume his complete insanity.

Puzzled, the ontologist gnawed his lower lip and stared at the message in the scriptor.

In his abstraction he found himself peering at the symbol "pi" in the scriptor message. *There,* at least, was something that had always been the same, and would endure for all time. He reached over to knock out his pipe in the big circular ash tray by the scriptor and paused in the middle of the second tap. From his desk he fished a tape measure and stretched it across the tray. Ten inches. And then around the circumference. Thirty-one and a half inches. Good enough, considering. It was a result any curious schoolboy could get.

He turned to the scriptor again.

"Memo to Math Section. Rush paragraph history on value of pi. Prentiss."

He didn't have to wait long.

> To Director: Re history "pi." Babylonians used value of 3.00. Aristotle made fairly accurate physical and theoretical evaluations. Archimedes first to arrive at modern value, using theory of limits. . . .

There was more, but it was lost on Prentiss. It was inconceivable, of course, that pi had grown during the two millenia that separated the Babylonians from Archimedes. And yet, it was exasperating. Why hadn't they done any better than 3.00? Any child with a piece of string could have demonstrated their error. Countless generations of wise, careful Chaldean astronomers, measuring time and star positions with such incredible accuracy, all coming to grief with a piece of string and pi. It didn't make sense. And certainly pi hadn't grown, any more than the Babylonian 360-day year had grown into the modern 365-day year. It had always been the same, he told himself. The primitives hadn't measured accurately, that was all. That *had* to be the explanation.

He hoped.

He sat down at his desk again, stared a moment at his memo pad and wrote:

> Check history of gravity—acceleration. Believe Aristotle unable detect acceleration. Galileo used same instruments, including same crude water clock, and found it. Why? . . . Any reported transits of Vulcan since 1914, when Einstein explained eccentricity of Mercury orbit by relativity instead of by hypothetical sunward planet? . . . How could Oliver Lodge detect an ether-drift and Michelson not? Conceivable that Lorentz contraction not a physical fact before Michelson experiment? . . . How many chemical elements were predicted before discovered?

He tapped absently on the pad a few times, then rang for a research assistant. He'd barely have time to explain what he wanted before he had to meet his class under Luce.

And he still wasn't sure where the rats fitted in.

CHAPTER THREE

CURTLY Professor Luce brought his address to a close.

"Well, gentlemen," he said, "I guess we'll have to continue this at our next lecture. We seem to have run over a little; class dismissed. Oh, Mr. Prentiss!"

The investigator looked up in genuine surprise. "Yes, sir?" The thin gun in his shoulder holster suddenly felt satisfyingly fat.

He realized that the crucial moment was near, that he would know before he left the campus whether this strange man was a harmless physicist, devoted to his lifework and his queer hobby, or whether he was an incarnate danger to mankind. The professor was acting out of turn, and it was an unexpected break.

"Mr. Prentiss," continued Luce from the lecture platform, "may I see you in my office a moment before you leave?"

Prentiss said, "Certainly." As the group broke up he followed the gaunt scientist through the door that led to Luce's little office behind the lecture room.

At the doorway he hesitated almost imperceptibly; Luce saw it and bowed sardonically. "After you, sir!"

Then the tall man indicated a chair near his desk. "Sit down, Mr. Prentiss."

For a long moment the seated men studied each other.

Finally the professor spoke. "About fifteen years ago a brilliant young man named Rogers wrote a doctoral dissertation at the University of Vienna on what he called . . . 'Involuntary Conformation of Incoming Sensoria to Apperception Mass.' "

Prentiss began fishing for his pipe. "Indeed?"

"One copy of the dissertation was sent to the Scholarship Society that was financing his studies. All others were seized by the International Bureau of the Censor, and accordingly a demand was made on the Scholarship Society for its copy. But it couldn't be found."

Prentiss was concentrating on lighting his pipe. He wondered if the faint trembling of the match flame was visible.

The professor turned to his desk, opened the top drawer, and pulled out a slim brochure bound in black leather.

The investigator coughed out a cloud of smoke.

The professor did not seem to notice, but opened the front cover and began reading: " '—a dissertation in partial fulfillment of the requirements for the degree of Doctor of Philosophy at the University of Vienna. A. P. Rogers, Vienna, 1957.' " The man closed the book and studied it thoughtfully. "Adam Prentiss Rogers—the owner of a brain whose like is seen not once in a century. He exposed the gods—then vanished."

Prentiss suppressed a shiver as he met those sunken, implacable eye-caverns.

The cat-and-mouse was over. In a way, he was relieved.

"Why did you vanish then, Mr. Prentiss-Rogers?" demanded Luce. "And why do you now reappear?"

The investigator blew a cloud of smoke toward the low ceiling. "To prevent people like you from introducing sensoria that *can't* be conformed to our present apperception mass. To keep reality as is. That answers both questions, I think."

The other man smiled. It was not a good thing to see. "Have you succeeded?"

"I don't know. So far, I suppose."

The gaunt man shrugged his shoulders. "You ignore tomorrow, then. I think you have failed, but I can't be sure, of course, until I actually perform the experiment that will create novel sensoria." He leaned forward. "I'll come to the point, Mr. Prentiss-Rogers. Next to yourself—and possibly excepting the Censor—I know more about the mathematical approach to reality than anyone else in the world. I may even know things about it that you don't. On other phases of it I'm weak—because I developed your results on the basis of mere logic rather than insight. And logic, we know, is applicable only within indeterminate limits. But in developing a practical device—an actual machine—for the wholesale alteration of incoming sensoria, I'm enormously ahead of you. You saw my apparatus last night, Mr. Prentiss-Rogers? Oh, come, don't be coy."

Prentiss drew deeply on his pipe.

"I saw it."

"Did you understand it?"

"No. It wasn't all there. At least, the apparatus on the table was incomplete. There's more to it than a Nicol prism and a goniometer."

"Ah, you are clever! Yes, I was wise in not permitting you to remain very long—no longer than necessary to whet your curiosity. Look, then! I offer you a partnership. Check my data and apparatus; in return you may be present when I run the experiment. We will attain enlightenment together. We will know all things. We will be gods!"

"And what about two billion other human beings?" said Prentiss, pressing softly at his shoulder holster.

The professor smiled faintly. "Their lunacy—assuming they continue to exist at all—may become slightly more pronounced, of course. But why worry about them?" The wolf-lip curled further. "Don't expect me to believe this aura of altruism, Mr. Prentiss-Rogers. I think you're afraid to face what lies behind our so-called 'reality.'"

"At least I'm a coward in a good cause." He stood up. "Have you any more to say?"

He knew that he was just going through the motions. Luce must have realized he had laid himself open to arrest half a dozen times in as many minutes: The bare possession of the missing copy of the dissertation, the frank admission of plans to experiment with reality and his attempted bribery of a high Censor official. And yet, the man's very bearing denied the possibility of being cut off in mid-career.

Luce's cheeks fluffed out in a brief sigh. "I'm sorry you can't be intelligent about this, Mr. Prentiss-Rogers. Yet, the time will come, you know, when you must make up your mind to go—*through,* shall we say? In fact, we may have to depend to a considerable degree on one another's companionship—*out there.* Even gods have to pass the time of day occasionally, and I have a suspicion that you and I are going to be quite chummy. So let us not part in enmity."

Prentiss' hand slid beneath his coat lapel and drew out the snub-nosed automatic. He had a grim foreboding that it was futile, and that the professor was laughing silently at him, but he had no choice.

"You are under arrest," he said unemotionally. "Come with me."

The other shrugged his shoulders, then something like a laugh, soundless in its mockery, surged up in his throat. "Certainly, Mr. Prentiss-Rogers."

He arose.

The room was plunged into instant blackness.

Prentiss fired three times, lighting up the gaunt chuckling form at each flash.

"Save your fire, Mr. Prentiss-Rogers. Lead doesn't get far in an intense diamagnetic screen. Study the magnetic damper on a lab balance the next time you're in the Censor Building!"

Somewhere a door slammed.

Several hours later Prentiss was eyeing his aide with ill-concealed distaste. Crush knew that he had been summoned by E to confer on the implications of Luce's escape, and that Crush was secretly sympathizing with him. Prentiss couldn't endure sympathy. He'd prefer that the asthmatic little man tell him how stupid he'd been.

"What do you want?" he growled.

"Sir," gasped Crush apologetically, "I have a report on that gadget you scanned in Luce's lab."

Prentiss was instantly mollified, but suppressed any show of interest. "What about it?"

"In essence, sir," wheezed Crush, "it's just a Nicol prism mounted on a goniometer. According to a routine check it was ground by an obscure optician who was nine years on the job, and he spent nearly all of that time on just one face of the prism. What do you make of that, sir?"

"Nothing, yet. What took him so long?"

"Grinding an absolutely flat edge, sir, so he says."

"Odd. That would mean a boundary composed exclusively of molecules of the same crystal layer, something that hasn't been attempted since the Palomar reflector."

"Yes, sir. And then there's a goniometer mount with

just one number on the dial—forty-five degrees."

"Obviously," said Prentiss, "the Nicol is to be used only at a forty-five degree angle to the incoming light. Hence it's probably extremely important—why, I don't know—that the angle be *precisely* forty-five degrees. That would require a perfectly flat surface, too, of course. I suppose you're going to tell me that the goniometric gearing is set up very accurately."

Suddenly Prentiss realized that Crush was looking at him in mingled suspicion and admiration.

"Well?" demanded the ontologist irritably. "Just what is the adjusting mechanism? Surely not geometrical? Too crude. Optical, perhaps?"

Crush gasped into his handkerchief. "Yes, sir. The prism is rotated very slowly into a tiny beam of light. Part of the beam is reflected and part refracted. At exactly forty-five degrees it seems, by Jordan's law, that exactly half is reflected and half refracted. The two beams are picked up in a photocell relay that stops the rotating mechanism as soon as the luminosities of the beams are exactly equal."

Prentiss tugged nervously at his ear. It was puzzling. Just what was Luce going to do with such an exquisitely-ground Nicol? At this moment he would have given ten years of his life for an inkling to the supplementary apparatus that went along with the Nicol. It would be something optical, certainly, tied in somehow with neurotic rats. What was it Luce had said the other night in the lab? Something about slowing down a photon. And then what was supposed to happen to the universe? Something like taking a tiny bite out of a balloon, Luce had said.

And how did it all interlock with certain impossible, though syllogistically necessary conclusions that flowed from his recent research into the history of human knowledge?

He wasn't sure. But he *was* sure that Luce was on the verge of using this mysterious apparatus to change the perceptible universe, on a scale so vast that humanity was going to get lost in the shuffle. He'd have to convince E of that.

If he couldn't he'd seek out Luce himself and kill him with his bare hands, and decide on reasons for it afterward.

He was guiding himself for the time being by pure insight, but he'd better be organized when he confronted E.

Crush was speaking. "Shall we go, sir? Your secretary says the jet is waiting." . . .

The painting showed a man in a red hat and black robes seated behind a high judge's bench. Five other men in red hats were seated behind a lower bench to his right, and four others to his left. At the base of the bench knelt a figure in solitary abjection.

"We condemn you, Galileo Galilei, to the formal prison of this Holy Office for a period determinable at Our pleasure; and by way of salutary penance, We order you, during the next three years, to recite once a week the seven Penitential Psalms."

Prentiss turned from the inscription to the less readable face of E. That oval olive-hued face was smooth, unlined, even around the eyes, and the black hair was parted off-center and drawn over the woman's head into a bun at the nape of her neck. She wore no make-up, and apparently needed none. She was clad in a black, loose-fitting business suit, which accentuated her perfectly moulded body.

"Do you know," said Prentiss coolly, "I think you like being Censor. It's in your blood."

"You're perfectly right. I *do* like being Censor. According to Speer, I effectively sublimate a guilt complex as strange as it is baseless."

"Very interesting. Sort of expiation of an ancestral guilt complex, eh?"

"What do you mean?"

"Woman started man on his acquisition of knowledge and self-destruction, and ever since has tried futilely to halt the avalanche. In you the feeling of responsibility and guilt runs exceptionally strong, and I'll wager that some nights you wake up in a cold sweat, thinking you've just plucked a certain forbidden fruit."

E stared icily up at the investigator's twitching mouth. "The only pertinent question," she said crisply, "is whether Luce is engaged in ontologic experiments, and if so, are they of a dangerous nature."

Prentiss sighed. "He's in it up to his neck. But just *what,* and how dangerous, I can only guess."

"Then guess."

"Luce thinks he's developed apparatus for the practical, predictable alteration of sensoria. He hopes to do something with his device that will blow physical laws straight to smithereens. The resulting reality would probably be recognizable even to a professional ontologist, let alone the mass of humanity."

"You seem convinced he can do this."

"The probabilities are high."

"Good enough. We can deal only in probabilities. The safest thing, of course, would be to locate Luce and kill him on sight. On the other hand, the faintest breath of scandal would result in Congressional hamstringing of the Bureau, so we must proceed cautiously."

"If Luce is really able to do what he claims," said Prentiss grimly, "and we let him do it, there won't be any Bureau at all—nor any Congress, either."

"I know. Rest assured that if I decide that Luce is dangerous and should die, I shall let neither the lives nor careers of anyone in the Bureau stand in the way, including myself."

Prentiss nodded, wondering if she really meant it.

The woman continued. "We are faced for the first time with a probable violation of our directive forbidding ontologic experiments. We are inclined to prevent this threatened violation by taking a man's life. I think we should settle once and for all whether such harsh measures are indicated, and it is for this that I have invited you to attend a staff conference. We intend to reopen the entire question of ontologic experiments and their implications."

Prentiss groaned inwardly. In matters so important the staff decided by vote. He had a brief vision of attempting to convince E's hard-headed scientists that mankind was changing "reality" from century to century—that not too long ago the earth had been "flat." Yes, by now he was beginning to believe it himself!

"Come this way, please?" said E.

CHAPTER FOUR

SITTING at E's right was an elderly man, Speer, the famous psychologist. On her left was Goring, staff advisor on nucleonics; next to him was Burchard, brilliant chemist and Director of the Western Field, then Prentiss, and then Dobbs, the renowned metallurgist and Director of the Central Field.

Prentiss didn't like Dobbs, who had voted against his promotion to the directorship of Eastern.

E announced: "We may as well start this inquiry with an examination of fundamentals. Mr. Prentiss, just what is reality?"

The ontologist winced. He had needed two hundred pages to outline the theory of reality in his doctoral thesis, and even so, had always suspected his examiners had passed it only because it was incomprehensible—hence a work of genius.

"Well," he began wryly, "I must confess that I don't know what *real* reality is. What most of us call reality is simply an integrated synthesis of incoming sensoria. As such it is nothing more than a working hypothesis in the mind of each of us, forever in a process of revision. In the past that process has been slow and safe. But we have now to consider the consequences of an instantaneous and total revision—a revision so far-reaching that it may thrust humanity face-to-face with the true reality, the world of Things-in-Themselves—Kant's *noumena*. This, I think, would be as disastrous as dumping a group of children in the middle of a forest. They'd have to relearn the simplest things—what to eat, how to protect themselves from elemental forces, and even a new language to deal with their new problems. There'd be few survivors.

"That is what we want to avoid, and we can do it if we prevent any sudden sweeping alteration of sensoria in our present reality."

He looked dubiously at the faces about him. It was a poor start. Speer's wrinkled features were drawn up in a serene smile, and the psychologist seemed to be contemplating the air over Prentiss' head. Goring was regarding him with grave, expressionless eyes. E nodded slightly as Prentiss' gaze travelled past her to a puzzled Burchard, thence to Dobbs, who was frankly contemptuous.

Speer and Goring were going to be the most susceptible. Speer because of his lack of a firm scientific background, Goring because nucleonics was in such a state of flux that nucleic experts were expressing the gravest doubts as to the validity of the laws worshipped by Burchard and Dobbs. Burchard was only a faint possibility. And Dobbs?

Dobbs said: "I don't know what the dickens you're talking about." The implication was plain that he wanted to add: "And I don't think you do, either."

And Prentiss wasn't so sure that he did know. Ontology was an elusive thing at best.

"I object to the term 'real reality,'" continued Dobbs. "A thing is real or it isn't. No fancy philosophical system can change *that*. And if it's real, it gives off predictable, reproducible sensory stimuli not subject to alteration except in the minds of lunatics."

Prentiss breathed more easily. His course was clear. He'd concentrate on Dobbs, with a little side-play on Burchard. Speer and Goring would never suspect his arguments were really directed at them. He pulled a gold coin from his vest pocket and slid it across the table to Dobbs, being careful not to let it clatter. "You're a metallurgist. Please tell us what this is."

Dobbs picked up the coin and examined it suspiciously. "It's quite obviously a five-dollar gold piece, minted at Fort Worth in Nineteen Sixty-Two. I can even give you the analysis, if you want it."

"I doubt that you could," said Prentiss coolly. "For you see, you are holding a counterfeit coin minted only last week in my own laboratories especially for this conference. As a matter of fact, if you'll forgive my saying so, I had you in mind when I ordered the coin struck. It contains no gold whatever—drop it on the table."

The coin fell from the fingers of the astounded metallurgist and clattered on the oaken table top.

"Hear the false ring?" demanded Prentiss.

Pink-faced, Dobbs cleared his throat and peered at the coin more closely. "How was I to know that? It's no disgrace, is it? Many clever counterfeits can be detected only in the laboratory. I knew the color was a little on the red side, but that could have been due to the lighting of the room. And of course, I hadn't given it an auditory test before I spoke. The ring is definitely dull. It's obviously a copper-lead alloy, with possibly a little amount of silver to help the ring. All right, I jumped to conclusions. So what? What does that prove?"

"It proves that you have arrived at two separate, distinct and mutually exclusive realities, starting with the same sensory premises. It proves how easily reality is revised. And that isn't all, as I shall soon—"

"All right," said Dobbs testily. "But on second thought I admitted it was a phony, didn't I?"

"Which demonstrates a further weakness in our routine acquisition and evaluation of pre-digested information. When an unimpeachable authority tells us something as a fact, we immediately, and without conscious thought, *modify* our incoming stimuli to conform with that *fact*. The coin suddenly acquires the red taint of copper, and rings false to the ear."

"I would have caught the queer ring anyhow," said Dobbs stubbornly, "with no help from 'an unimpeachable authority.' The ring would have sounded the same, no matter what you said."

From the corner of his eye Prentiss noticed that Speer was grinning broadly. Had the old psychologist divined his trick? He'd take a chance.

"Dr. Speer," he said, "I think you have something interesting to tell our doubting friend."

Speer cackled dryly. "You've been a perfect guinea pig, Dobbsie. The coin was genuine."

The metallurgist's jaw dropped as he looked blankly from one face to another. Then his jowls slowly grew red. He flung the coin to the table. "Maybe I am a guinea pig. I'm a realist, too. I think this is a piece of metal. You might fool me as to its color or assay, but in essence and substance, it's a piece of metal." He glared at Prentiss and Speer in turn. "Does anyone deny that?"

"Certainly not," said Prentiss. "Our mental pigeonholes are identical in that respect; they accept the same sensory definition of 'piece of metal,' or 'coin.' Whatever this object is, it emits stimuli that our minds are capable of registering and abstracting as a 'coin.' But note: we make a coin out of it. However, if I could shuffle my cortical pigeonholes, I might find it to be a chair, or a steamer trunk, possibly with Dr. Dobbs inside, or, if the shuffling were extreme, there might be no semantic pattern into which the incoming stimuli could be routed. There wouldn't be anything there at all!"

"Sure," sneered Dobbs. "You could walk right through it."

"Why not?" asked Prentiss gravely. "I think we may do it all the time. Matter is about the emptiest stuff imaginable. If you compressed that coin to eliminate the space between its component atoms and electrons, you couldn't see it in a microscope."

Dobbs stared at the enigmatic goldpiece as though it might suddenly thrust out a pseudopod and swallow him up. Then he said flatly: "No. I don't believe it. It exists as a coin, and only as a coin—whether I know it or not."

"Well," ventured Prentiss, "how about you, Dr. Goring? Is the coin real to you?"

The nucleist smiled and shrugged his shoulders. "If I don't think too much about it, it's real enough. And yet..."

Dobbs's face clouded. "And yet what? Here it is. Can you doubt the evidence of your own eyes?"

"That's just the difficulty." Goring leaned forward. "My eyes tell me, here's a coin. Theory tells me, here's a mass of hypothetical disturbances in a hypothetical subether in a hypothetical ether. The indeterminacy principle tells me that I can never know both the mass and position of these hypothetical disturbances. And as a physicist I know that the bare fact of observing something is sufficient to change that something from its pre-observed state. Nevertheless, I compromise by letting my senses and practical experience stick a tag on this particular bit of the unknowable. X, after its impact on my mind (whatever *that* is!) equals coin. A single equation with two variables has no solution. The best I can say is, it's a coin, but probably not really—"

"Hah!" declared Burchard. "I can demonstrate the fallacy of *that* position very quickly. If our minds make this a coin, then our minds make this little object an ashtray, that a window, the thing that holds us up, a chair. You might say we make the air we breathe, and perhaps even the stars and planets. Why, following Prentiss' idea to its logical end, the universe itself is the work of man—a conclusion I'm sure he doesn't intend."

"Oh, but I do," said Prentiss.

Prentiss took a deep breath. The issue could be dodged no longer. He had to take a stand. "And to make sure you understand me, whether you agree with me or not, I'll state categorically that I believe the apparent universe to be the work of man."

Even E looked startled, but said nothing.

The ontologist continued rapidly. "All of you doubt my sanity. A week ago I would have, too. But since then I've done a great deal of research in the history of science. And I repeat, *the universe is the work of man*. I believe that man began his existence in some incredibly simple world—the original and true *noumenon* of our present universe. And that over the centuries man expanded his little world into its present vastness and incomprehensible intricacy solely by dint of imagination.

"Consequently, I believe that what most of you call the 'real' world has been changing ever since our ancestors began to think."

Dobbs smiled superciliously. "Oh, come now, Prentiss. That's just a rhetorical description of scientific progress over the past centuries. In the same sense I might say that modern transportation and communications have shrunk the earth. But you'll certainly admit that the physical state of things has been substantially constant ever since the galaxies formed and the earth began to cool, and that the simple cosmologies of early man were simply the result of lack of means for obtaining accurate information?"

"I *won't* admit it," rejoined Prentiss bluntly. "I maintain that their information was substantially accurate. I maintain that at one time in our history the earth was flat—as flat as it is now round, and no one living before the time of Hecataeus, though he might have been equipped with the finest modern instruments, could have proved otherwise. His mind was *conditioned* to a two-dimensional world. Any of us present, if we were transplanted to the world of Hecataeus, could, of course, establish terrestrial sphericity in short order. Our minds have been conditioned to a three-dimensional world. The day may come a few millennia hence when a four-dimensional Terra will be commonplace even to schoolchildren; they will have been intuitively conditioned in relativistic concepts." He added slyly: "And the less intelligent of them may attempt to blame our naïve three-dimensional planet on our grossly inaccurate instruments, because it will be as plain as day to them that their planet has four dimensions!"

CHAPTER FIVE

DOBBS snorted at this amazing idea. The other scientists stared at Prentiss with an awe which was mixed with incredulity.

Goring said cautiously: "I follow up to a certain point. I can see that a primitive society might start out with a limited number of facts. They would offer theories to harmonize and integrate those facts, and then those first theories would require that new, additional facts exist, and in their search for those secondary facts, extraneous data would turn up inconsistent with the first theories. Secondary theories would then be required, from which hitherto unguessed facts should follow, the confirmation of which would discover more inconsistencies. So the pattern of fact to theory to fact to theory, and so on, finally brings us into our present state of knowledge. Does that follow from your argument?"

Prentiss nodded.

"But won't you admit that the facts were there all the time, and merely awaited discovery?"

"The simple, unelaborated *noumenon* was there all the time, yes. But the new fact—man's new interpretation of the *noumenon,* was generally pure invention—a mental creation, if you like. This will be clearer if you consider how rarely a new fact arises before a theory exists for its explanation. In the ordinary scientific investigation, theory comes first, followed in short order by the 'discovery' of various facts deducible from it."

Goring still looked sceptical. "But that wouldn't mean the fact wasn't there all the time."

"Wouldn't it? Look at the evidence. Has it never struck you as odd in how many instances very obvious facts were 'overlooked' until a theory was propounded that required their existence? Take your nuclear building blocks. Protons and electrons were detected physically only after Rutherford had showed they had to exist. And then when Rutherford found that protons and electrons were not enough to build all the atoms of the periodic table, he postulated the neutron, which of course was duly 'discovered' in the Wilson cloud chamber."

Goring pursed his lips. "But the Wilson cloud chamber would have shown all that prior to the theory, if anyone had only thought to use it. The mere fact that Wilson didn't invent his cloud chamber until Nineteen Twelve and Geiger didn't invent his counter until Nineteen Thirteen, would not keep sub-atomic particles from existing before that time."

"You don't get the point," said Prentiss. "The primitive, ungeneralized *noumenon* that we today observe as sub-atomic particles existed prior to Nineteen Twelve, true, *but not sub-atomic particles.*"

"Well, I don't know. . . ." Goring scratched his chin. "How about fundamental forces? Surely electricity existed before Galvani? Even the Greeks knew how to build up electrostatic charges on amber."

"Greek electricity was nothing more than electrostatic charges. Nothing more could be created until Galvani introduced the concept of the electric current."

"Do you mean the electric current didn't exist at all before Galvani?" demanded Burchard. "Not even when lightning struck a conductor?"

"Not even then. We don't know much about pre-Galvanic lightning. While it probably packed a wallop, its destructive potential couldn't have been due to its delivery of an electric current. The Chinese flew kites for centuries before Franklin theorized that lightning was the same as galvanic electricity, but there's no recorded shock from a kite string until our learned statesman drew forth one in Seventeen Sixty-five. *Now*, only an idiot flies a kite in a storm. It's all according to pattern: theory first, then we alter 'reality' to fit."

Burchard persisted. "Then I suppose you'd say the ninety-two elements are figments of our imagination."

"Correct," agreed Prentiss. "I believe that in the beginning there were only four *noumenal* elements. Man simply elaborated these according to the needs of his growing science. Man made them what they are today—and on occasion, *unmade* them. You remember the havoc Mendelyeev created with his periodic law. He declared that the elements had to follow valence sequences of increasing atomic weight, and when they didn't, he insisted his law was right and that the atomic weights were wrong. He must have had Stas and Berzelius whirling in their graves, because they had worked out the 'erroneous' atomic weights with marvellous precision. The odd thing was, when the weights were rechecked, they fitted the Mendelyeev table. But that wasn't all. The old rascal pointed out vacant spots in his table and maintained that there were more elements yet to be discovered. He even perdicted what properties they'd have. He was too modest. I state that Nilson, Winkler, and De Boisbaudran merely *discovered* scandium, germanium, and gallium; Mendelyeev *created* them, out of the original tetraelemental stuff."

E leaned forward. "That's a bit strong. Tell me, if man has changed the elements and the cosmos to suit his convenience, what was the cosmos like before man came on the scene?"

"There wasn't any," answered Prentiss. "Remember, by defintion, 'cosmos' or 'reality' is simply man's version of the ultimate *noumenal* universe. The 'cosmos' arrives and departs with the mind of man. Consequently, the earth—as such—didn't even exist before the advent of man."

"But the evidence of the rocks . . ." protested E. "Pressures applied over millions, even billions of years, were needed to form them, unless you postulate an omnipotent God who called them into existence as of yesterday."

"I postulate only the omnipotent human mind," said

Prentiss. "In the Seventeenth Century, Hooke, Ray, Woodward, to name a few, studied chalk, gravel, marble, and even coal, without finding anything inconsistent with results to be expected from the Noachian Flood. But now that we've made up our minds that the earth is older, the rocks *seem* older, too."

"But how about evolution?" demanded Burchard. "Surely that wasn't a matter of a few centuries?"

"Really?" replied Prentiss. "Again, why assume that the facts are any more recent than the theory? The evidence is all the other way. Aristotle was a magnificent experimental biologist, and he was convinced that life could be created spontaneously. Before the time of Darwin there was no need for the various species to evolve, because they sprang into being from inanimate matter. As late as the Eighteenth Century, Needham, using a microscope, reported that he saw microbe life arise spontaneously out of sterile culture media. These abiogeneticists were, of course, discredited and their work found to be irreproducible, but only *after* it became evident that the then abiogenetic facts were going to run inconsistent with later 'facts' flowing from advancing biologic theory."

"Then," said Goring, "assuming purely for the sake of argument, that man has altered the original *noumena* into our present reality, just what danger do you think Luce represents to that reality? How could he do anything about it, even if he wanted to? Just what is he up to?"

"Broadly stated," said Prentiss, "Luce intends to destroy the Einsteinian universe."

Burchard frowned and shook his head. "Not so fast. In the first place, how can anyone presume to destroy this planet, much less the whole universe? And why do you say the 'Einsteinian' universe? The universe by any other name is still the universe, isn't it?"

"What Dr. Prentiss means," explained E, "is that Luce wants to revise completely and finally our present comprehension of the universe, which presently happens to be the Einsteinian version, in the expectation that the final version would be the true one—and comprehensible only to Luce and perhaps a few other ontologic experts."

"I don't see it," said Dobbs irritably. "Apparently this

Luce contemplates nothing more than publication of a new scientific theory. How can that be bad? A mere theory can't hurt anybody—especially if only two or three people understand it."

"You—and two billion others," said Prentiss softly, "think that 'reality' cannot be affected by any theory that seems to change it—that it is optional with you to accept or reject the theory. In the past that was true. If the Ptolemaics wanted a geocentric universe, they ignored Copernicus. If the four-dimensional continuum of Einstein and Minkowsky seemed incomprehensible to the Newtonian school they dismissed it, and the planets continued to revolve substantially as Newton predicted. But this is different.

"For the first time we are faced with the probability that the promulgation of a theory is going to *force* an ungaspable reality upon our minds. It will not be optional."

"Well," said Burchard, "if by 'promulgation of a theory' you mean something like the application of the quantum theory and relativity to the production of atomic energy, which of course has changed the shape of civilization in the past generation, whether the individual liked it or not, then I can understand you. But if you mean that Luce is going to make one little experiment that may confirm some new theory or other, and *ipso facto* and instantaneously reality is going to turn topsy turvy, why I say it's nonsense."

"Would anyone," said Prentiss quietly, "care to guess what would happen if Luce were able to destroy a photon?"

Goring laughed shortly. "The question doesn't make sense. The mass-energy entity whose three-dimensional profile we call a photon is indestructible."

"But if you *could* destroy it?" insisted Prentiss. "What would the universe be like afterward?"

"What difference would it make?" demanded Dobbs. "One photon more or less?"

"Plenty," said Goring. "According to the Einstein theory, every particle of matter-energy has a gravitational potential, lambda, and it can be calculated that the total lambdas are precisely sufficient to keep our four-dimensional continuum from closing back on itself. Take one lambda away—my heavens! The universe would split wide open!"

"Exactly," said Prentiss. "Instead of a continuum, our 'reality' would become a disconnected *mélange* of three-dimensional objects. Time, if it existed, wouldn't bear any relation to spatial things. Only an ontologic expert might be able to synthesize any sense out of such a 'reality.'"

"Well," said Dobbs, "I wouldn't worry too much. I don't think anybody's ever going to destroy a photon." He snickered. "You have to catch one first!"

"Luce can catch one," said Prentiss calmly. "And he can destroy it. At this moment some unimaginable post-Einsteinian universe lies in the palm of his hand. Final, true reality, perhaps. But we aren't ready for it. Kant, perhaps, or *homo superior,* but not the general run of *h. sapiens*. We wouldn't be able to escape our conditioning. We'd be stopped cold."

He stopped. Without looking at Goring, he knew he had convinced the man. Prentiss sagged with visible relief. It was time for a vote. He must strike before Speer and Goring could change their minds.

"Madame"—he shot a questioning glance at the woman—"at any moment my men are going to report that they've located Luce. I must be ready to issue the order for his execution, if in fact the staff believes such disposition proper. I call for a vote of officers!"

"Granted," said E instantly. "Will those in favor of destroying Luce on sight raise their right hands?"

Prentiss and Goring made the required signal.

Speer was silent.

Prentiss felt his heart sinking. Had he made a gross error of judgment?

"I vote against this murder," declared Dobbs. "That's what it is, pure murder."

"I agree with Dobbs," said Burchard shortly.

All eyes were on the psychologist. "I presume you'll join us, Dr. Speer?" demanded Dobbs sternly.

"Count me out, gentlemen. I'd never interfere with anything so inevitable as the destiny of man. All of you are overlooking a fundamental facet of human nature—man's insatiable hunger for change, novelty—for anything different from what he already has. Prentiss himself states that whenever man grows discontented with his present reality, he starts elaborating it, and the devil take the hindmost. Luce but symbolizes the evil genius of our race—and I mean both our species and the race toward intertwined godhood and destruction. Once born, however, symbols are immortal. It's far too late now to start killing Luces. It was too late when the first man tasted the first apple.

"Furthermore, I think Prentiss greatly overestimates the scope of Luce's pending victory over the rest of mankind. Suppose Luce is actually successful in clearing space and time and suspending the world in the temporal statis of its present irreality. Suppose he and a few ontologic experts pass on into the ultimate, true reality. How long do you think they can resist the temptation to alter it? If Prentiss is right, eventually they or their descendants will be living in a cosmos as intricate and unpleasant as the one they left, while we, for all practical purposes, will be pleasantly dead.

"No gentlemen, I won't vote either way."

"Then it is my privilege to break the tie," said E coolly. "I vote for death. Save your remonstrances, Dr. Dobbs. It's after midnight. This meeting is adjourned." She stood up in abrupt dismissal, and the men were soon filing from the room.

E left the table and walked toward the windows on the far side of the room. Prentiss hesitated a moment, but made no effort to leave.

E called over her shoulder, "You, too, Prentiss."

The door closed behind Speer, the last of the group, save Prentiss.

Prentiss walked up behind E.

She gave no sign of awareness.

Six feet away, the man stopped and studied her.

Sitting, walking, standing, she was lovely. Mentally he compared her to Velasquez' Venus. There was the same slender exquisite proportion of thigh, hip, and bust. And he knew she was completely aware of her own beauty, and further, must be aware of his present appreciative scrutiny.

Then her shoulders sagged suddenly, and her voice seemed very tired when she spoke. "So you're still here, Prentiss. Do you believe in intuition?"

"Not often."

"Speer was right. He's always right. Luce will succeed." She dropped her arms to her sides and turned.

"Then may I reiterate, my dear, marry me and let's forget the control of knowledge for a few months."

"Completely out of the question, Prentiss. Our natures are incompatible. You're incorrigibly curious, and I'm incorrigibly, even neurotically, conservative. Besides, how can you even think about such things when we've got to stop Luce?"

His reply was interrupted by the shrilling of the intercom: "Calling Mr. Prentiss. Crush calling Mr. Prentiss. Luce located. Crush calling."

CHAPTER SIX

WITH his pencil Crush pointed to a shaded area of the map. "This is Luce's Snake-Eyes estate, the famous game preserve and zoo. Somewhere in the centre—about here, I think—is a stone cottage. A moving van unloaded some lab equipment there this morning."

"Mr. Prentiss," said E, "how long do you think it will take him to install what he needs for that one experiment?"

The ontologist answered from across the map table. "I can't be sure. I still have no idea of what he's going to try, except that I'm reasonably certain it must be done in absolute darkness. Checking his instruments will require but a few minutes at most."

The woman began pacing the floor nervously. "I knew it. We can't stop him. We have no time."

"Oh, I don't know," said Prentiss. "How about that stone cottage, Crush? Is it pretty old?"

"Dates from the Eighteenth Century, sir."

"There's your answer," said Prentiss. "It's probably full

of holes where the mortar's fallen out. For total darkness he'll have to wait until moonset."

"That's three thirty-four a.m., sir," said Crush.

"We've time for an arrest," said E.

Crush looked dubious. "It's more complicated than that, Madame. Snake-Eyes is fortified to withstand a small army. Luce could hold off any force the Bureau could muster for at least twenty-four hours."

"One atom egg, well done," suggested Prentiss.

"That's the best answer, of course," agreed E. "But you know as well as I what the reaction of Congress would be to such extreme measures. There would be an investigation. The Bureau would be abolished, and all persons responsible for such an expedient would face life imprisonment, perhaps death." She was silent for a moment, then sighed and said: "So be it. If there is no alternative, I shall order the bomb dropped."

"There may be another way," said Prentiss.

"Indeed?"

"Granted an army couldn't get through. One man might. And if he made it, you could call off your bomb."

E exhaled a slow cloud of smoke and studied the glowing tip of her cigarette. Finally she turned and looked into the eyes of the ontologist for the first time since the beginning of the conference. "*You* can't go."

"Who, then?"

Her eyes dropped. "You're right, of course. But the bomb still falls if you don't get through. It's got to be that way. Do you understand that?"

Prentiss laughed. "I understand."

He addressed his aide. "Crush, I'll leave the details up to you, bomb and all. We'll rendezvous at these coordinates"—he pointed to the map—"at three sharp. It's after one now. You'd better get started."

"Yes, sir," wheezed Crush, and scurried out of the room.

As the door closed, Prentiss turned to E. "Beginning tomorrow afternoon—or rather, *this* afternoon, after I finish with Luce, I want six months off."

"Granted," murmured E.

"I want you to come with me. I want to find out just what this thing is between us. Just the two of us. It may take a little time."

E smiled crookedly. "If we're both still alive at three thirty-five, and such a thing as a month exists, and you still want me to spend six of them with you, I'll do it. And in return you can do something for me."

"What?"

"You, even above Luce, stand the best chance of adjusting to final reality if Luce is successful in destroying a photon. I'm a borderline case. I'm going to need all the help you can give me, if and when the time comes. Will you remember that?"

"I'll remember," Prentiss said.

At 3 a.m. he joined Crush.

"There are at least seven infra-red scanners in the grounds, sir," said Crush, "not to mention an intricate network of photo relays. And then the **wire** fence around the lab, with the big cats inside. He must have turned the whole zoo loose." The little man reluctantly helped Prentiss into his infra-red absorbing coveralls. "You weren't meant for tiger fodder, sir. Better call it off."

Prentiss zipped up his visor and grimaced out into the moonlit dimness of the apple orchard. "You'll take care of the photocell network?"

"Certainly, sir. He's using u.v.-sensitive cells. We'll blanket the area with a u.v.-spot at three-ten."

Prentiss strained his ears, but couldn't hear the 'copter that would carry the u.v.-searchlight—and the bomb.

"It'll be here, sir," Crush assured him. "It won't make any noise, anyhow. What you ought to be worrying about are those wild beasts."

The investigator sniffed at the night air. "Darn little breeze."

"Yeah," gasped Crush. "And variable at that, sir. You can't count on going in upwind. You want us to create a diversion at one end of the grounds to attract the animals?"

"We don't dare. If necessary, I'll open the aerosol capsule of formaldehyde." He held out his hand. "Goodbye, Crush."

His asthmatic assistant shook the extended hand with vigorous sincerity. "Good luck, sir. And don't forget the bomb. We'll have to drop it at three thirty-four sharp."

But Prentiss had vanished into the leafy darkness.

A little later he was studying the luminous figures on his watch. The u.v.-blanket was presumably on. All he had to be careful about in the next forty seconds was a direct collision with a photocell post.

But Crush's survey party had mapped well. He reached the barbed fencing uneventfully, with seconds to spare. He listened a moment, and then in practiced silence eased his lithe body high up and over.

The breeze, which a moment before had been in his face, now died away, and the night air hung about him in dark lifeless curtains.

From the stone building a scant two hundred yards ahead, a chink of light peeped out.

Prentiss drew his silenced pistol and began moving forward with swift caution, taking care to place his heel to ground before the toe, and feeling out the character of the ground with the thin soles of his sneakers before each step. A snapping twig might hurl a slavering wild beast at his throat.

He stopped motionless in midstride.

From a thicket several yards to his right came an ominous snuffing, followed by a low snarl.

His mouth went suddenly dry as he strained his ears and turned his head slowly toward the sound.

And then there came the reverberations of something heavy, hurtling toward him.

The great cat was almost upon him before he fired, and then the faint cough of the stumbling, stricken animal seemed louder than his muffled shot.

Breathing hard, Prentiss stepped away from the dying beast, evidently a panther, and listened for a long time before resuming his march on the cottage. Luce's extraordinary measures to exclude intruders but confirmed his suspicions: Tonight was the last night that the professor could be stopped. He blinked the stinging sweat from his eyes and glanced at his watch. It was 3.15.

Apparently the other animals had not heard him. He stood up to resume his advance, and to his utter relief found that the wind had shifted almost directly into his face and was blowing steadily.

In another three minutes he was standing at the massive door of the building, running practiced fingers over the great iron hinges and lock. Undoubtedly the thing was going to squeak; there was no time to apply oil and wait for it to soak in. The lock could be easily picked.

And the squeaking of a rusty hinge was probably immaterial. A cunning operator like Luce would undoubtedly have wired an alarm into it. He just couldn't believe Crush's report to the contrary.

But he couldn't stand here.

There was only one way to get inside quickly, and alive.

Chuckling at his own madness, Prentiss began to pound on the door.

He could visualize the blinking out of the slit of light above his head, and knew that, somewhere within the building, two flame-lit eyes were studying him in an infra-red scanner.

Prentiss tried simultaneously to listen to the muffled squeaking of the rats beyond the great door and to the swift, padding approach of something big behind him.

"Luce?" he cried. "It's Prentiss! Let me in!"

A latch slid somewhere; the door eased inward. The investigator threw his gun rearward at a pair of bounding eyes, laced his fingers over his head, and stumbled into more darkness.

Despite the protection of his hands, the terrific blow of the blackjack on his temple almost knocked him out.

He closed his eyes, crumpled carefully to the floor, and noted with satisfaction that his wrists were being tied behind his back. As he had anticipated, it was a clumsy job, even without his imperceptible "assistance." Long fingers ran over his body in a search for more weapons.

Then he felt the sting of a hypodermic needle in his biceps.

The lights came on.

He struggled feebly, emitted a plausible groan, and tried to sit up.

From far above, the strange face of Dr. Luce looked down at him, illuminated, it seemed to Prentiss, by some unhallowed inner fire.

"What time is it?" asked Prentiss.

"Approximately three-twenty."

"*Hm.* Your kittens gave me quite a reception, my dear professor."

"As befits an unco-operative meddler."

"Well, what are you going to do with me?"

"Kill you."

Luce pulled a pistol from his coat pocket.

Prentiss wet his lips. During his ten years with the Bureau, he had never had to deal with anyone quite like Luce. The gaunt man personified megalomania on a scale beyond anything the investigator had previously encountered—or imagined possible.

And, he realized with a shiver, Luce was very probably justified in his prospects (not delusions!) of grandeur.

With growing alarm he watched Luce snap off the safety lock of the pistol.

There were two possible chances of surviving more than a few seconds.

Luce's index finger began to tense around the trigger.

One of those chances was to appeal to Luce's megalomania, treating him as a human being. Tell him, "I know you won't kill me until you've had a chance to gloat over me—to tell me, the inventor of ontologic synthesis, how you found a practical application of it."

No good. Too obvious to one of Luce's intelligence.

The approach must be to a demi-god, in humility. Oddly enough his curiosity *was* tinged with respect. Luce *did* have something.

Prentiss licked his lips again and said hurriedly: "I must die, then. But could you show me—is it asking too much to show me, just how you propose to 'go through'?"

The gun lowered a fraction of an inch. Luce eyed the doomed man suspiciously.

"Would you, please?" continued Prentiss. His voice was dry, cracking. "Ever since I discovered that new realities could be synthesized, I've wondered whether *homo sapiens* was capable of finding a practical device for uncovering the true reality. And all who've worked on it have insisted that only a brain but little below the angels was capable of such an achievement." He coughed apologetically. "It is difficult to believe that a mere mortal has really accomplished what you claim—and yet, there's something about you . . ." His voice trailed off, and he laughed deprecatingly.

Luce bit; he thrust the gun back into his coat pocket. "So you know when you're licked," he sneered. "Well, I'll let you live a moment longer."

He stepped back and pulled aside a black screen. "Has the inimitable ontologist the wit to understand this?"

Within a few seconds of his introduction to the instrument everything was painfully clear. Prentiss now abandoned any remote hope that either Luce's method or apparatus would prove faulty. Both the vacuum-glassed machinery and the idea behind it were perfect.

Basically, the supplementary unit, which he now saw for the first time, consisted of a sodium-vapour light bulb, blacked out except for one tiny transparent spot. Ahead of the little window was a series of what must be hundreds of black discs mounted on a common axis. Each disc bore a slender radial slot. And though he could not trace all the gearing, Prentiss knew that the discs were geared to permit one and only one fleeting photon of yellow light to emerge at the end of the disc series, where it would pass through a Kerr electro-optic field and be polarized.

That photon would then travel one centimetre to that fabulous Nicol prism, one surface of which had been machined flat to a molecule's thickness. That surface was turned by means of an equally marvellous goniometer to meet the oncoming photon at an angle of exactly 45 degrees. And then would come chaos.

The cool voice of E sounded in his ear receptor. "Prentiss, it's three-thirty. If you understand the apparatus, and find it dangerous, will you so signify? If possible, describe it for the tapes."

"I understand your apparatus perfectly," said Prentiss.

Luce grunted, half irritated, half curious.

Prentiss continued hurriedly. "Shall I tell you how you decided upon this specific apparatus?"

"If you think you can."

"You have undoubtedly seen the sun reflect from the surface of the sea."

Luce nodded.

"But the fish beneath the surface see the sun, too," continued Prentiss. "Some of the photons are reflected and reach you, and some are refracted and reach the fish. But, for a given wave length, the photons are identical. Why should one be absorbed and another reflected?"

"You're on the right track," admitted Luce, "but couldn't you account for their behavior by Jordan's law?"

"Statistically, yes. Individually, no. In Nineteen Thirty-

136

four Jordan showed that a beam of polarized light splits up when it hits a Nicol prism. He proved that when the prism forms an angle, alpha, with the plane of polarization of the prism, a fraction of the light equal to $\cos^2$alpha passes through the prism, and the remainder, $\sin^2$alpha, is reflected. For example, if alpha is 60 degrees, three-fourths of the photons are reflected and one-fourth are refracted. But note that Jordan's law applied only to streams of photons, and you're dealing with a single photon, to which you're presenting an angle of exactly 45°. And how does a single photon make up its mind—or the photonic equivalent of a mind—when the probability of reflecting is exactly equal to the probability of refracting? Of course, if our photon is but one little mote along with billions of others, the whole comprising a light beam, we can visualize orders left for him by a sort of statistical traffic keeper stationed somewhere in the beam. A member of a beam, it may be presumed, has a pretty good idea of how many of his brothers have already reflected, and how many refracted, and hence knows which he must do."

"But suppose our single photon isn't in a beam at all?" said Luce.

"Your apparatus," said Prentiss, "is going to provide just such a photon. And I think it will be a highly confused little photon, just as your experimental rat was, that night not so long ago. I think it was Schroedinger who said that these physical particles were startlingly human in many of their aspects. Yes, your photon will be given a choice of equal probability. Shall he reflect? Shall he refract? The chances are 50 per cent for either choice. He will have no reason for selecting one in preference to the other. There will have been no swarm of preceding photons to set up a traffic guide for him. He'll be puzzled; and trying to meet a situation for which he has no proper response; he'll slow down. And when he does, he'll cease to be a photon, which must travel at the speed of light or cease to exist. Like your rat, like many human beings, he solves the unsolvable by disintegrating."

Luce said: "And when it disintegrates, there disappears one of the lambdas that hold together the Einstein space-time continuum. And when *that* goes, what's left can be only final reality untainted by theory or imagination. Do you see any flaw in my plan?"

CHAPTER SEVEN

TUGGING with subtle quickness on the cords that bound him, Prentiss knew there was no flaw in the man's reasoning, and that every human being on earth was now living on borrowed time.

He could think of no way to stop him; there remained only the bare threat of the bomb.

He said tersely: "If you don't submit to peaceable arrest within a few seconds, an atom bomb is going to be dropped on this area."

Sweat was getting into his eyes again, and he winked rapidly.

Luce's dark features convulsed, hung limp, then coalesced into a harsh grin. "She'll be too late," he said with grim good humor. "Her ancestors tried for centuries to thwart mine. But we were successful—always. Tonight I succeed again, and for all time."

Prentiss had one hand free.

In seconds he would be at the man's throat. He worked with quiet fury at the loops around his bound wrist.

Again E's voice in his ear receptor. "I had to do it!" The tones were strangely sad, self-accusing, remorseful.

Had to do *what*?

And his dazed mind was trying to digest the fact that E had just destroyed him.

She was continuing. "The bomb was dropped ten seconds ago." She was almost pleading, and her words were running together. "You were helpless; you couldn't kill him. I had a sudden premonition of what the world would be like—afterward—even for those who go through. Forgive me."

Almost mechanically he resumed his fumbling with the cord.

Luce looked up. "What's that?"

"What?" asked Prentiss dully. "I don't hear anything."

"Of course you do! Listen!"

The wrist came free.

Several things happened.

That faraway shriek in the skies grew into a howling crescendo of destruction.

As one man Prentiss and Luce leaped toward the activator switches. Luce got there first—an infinitesimal fraction of time before the walls were completely disintegrated.

There was a brief, soundless interval of utter blackness.

And then it seemed to Prentiss that a titanic stone wall crashed into his brain, and held him, mute, immobile.

But he was not dead.

For the name of this armored, stunning wall was not the bomb, but Time itself.

He knew in a brief flash of insight, that for sentient, thinking beings, Time had suddenly become a barricade rather than an endless road.

The exploding bomb—the caving cottage walls—were hanging, somewhere, frozen fast in an immutable, eternal stasis.

Luce had separated this fleeting unseen dimension from the creatures and things that had flowed along it. There is no existence without change along a temporal continuum. And now the continuum had been shattered.

Was this, then, the fate of all tangible things—of all humanity?

Were none of them—not even the two or three who understood advanced ontology, to—get through?

There was nothing but a black, eerie silence all around.

His senses were useless.

He even doubted he had any senses.

So far as he could tell he was nothing but an intelligence, floating in space. But he couldn't even be sure of *that*. Intelligence—space—they weren't necessarily the same now as before.

All that he knew for sure was that he doubted. He doubted everything except the fact of doubting.

Shades of Descartes!

To doubt is to think!

Ergo sum!

I exist.

Instantly he was wary. He existed, but not necessarily as Adam Prentiss Rogers. For the *noumenon* of Adam Prentiss Rogers might be—whom?

But he was safe. He was going to get through.

Relax, be resilient, he urged his whirling brain. You're on the verge of something marvellous.

It seemed that he could almost hear himself talk, and he was glad. A voiceless final reality would have been unbearable.

He essayed a tentative whisper:

"E!"

From somewhere far away a woman whimpered.

He cried eagerly into the blackness. "Is that you?"

Something unintelligible and strangely frightening answered him.

"Don't try to hold on to yourself," he cried. "Just let yourself go! Remember, you won't be E any more, but the *noumenon*, the essence of E. Unless you change enough to permit your *noumenon* to take over your old identity, you'll have to stay behind."

There was a groan. "But I'm *me*!"

"But you *aren't*—not really," he pleaded quickly. "You're just an aspect of a larger, symbolical *you*—the *noumenon* of E. It's yours for the asking. You have only to hold out your hand to grasp the shape of final reality. And you *must,* or cease to exist!"

A wail: "But what will happen to my body?"

The ontologist almost laughed. "I wouldn't know; but if it changes, I'll be sorrier than you!"

There was a silence.

"E!" he called.

No answer.

"E! Did you get through? *E!*"

The empty echoes skirled between the confines of his narrow blackness.

Had the woman lost even her struggling interstitial existence? Whenever, whatever, or wherever she now was, he could no longer detect.

Somehow, if it had ever come to this, he had counted on her being with him—just the two of them.

In stunned uneasy wonder he considered what his existence was going to be like from now on.

And what about Luce?

Had the demonic professor possessed sufficient mental elasticity to slip through?

And if so, just what was the professorial *noumenon* —the real Luce—like?

He'd soon know.

The ontologist relaxed again, and began floating through a dreamy patch of light and darkness. A pale glow began gradually to form about his eyes, and shadowy things began to form, dissolve, and reform.

He felt a great rush of gratitude. At least the shape of final reality was to be visible.

And then, at about the spot where Luce had stood, he saw the Eyes—two tiny red flames, transfixing him with unfathomable fury.

The same eyes that had burned into his that night of his first search!

Luce had got through—but wait!

An unholy aura was playing about the sinuous shadow that contained the jewelled flames. Those eyes were brilliant, horrid facets of hate in the head of a huge, coiling serpent-thing! Snake-Eyes!

In mounting awe and fear the ontologist understood that Luce had not got through—as Luce. That the *noumenon,* the essence, of Luce—was nothing human. That Luce, the bearer of light, aspirant to godhood, was not just Luce!

By the faint light he began shrinking away from the coiled horror, and in the act saw that *he,* at least, still had a human body. He knew this, because he was completely nude.

He was still human, and the snake-creature wasn't —and therefore never had been.

Then he noticed that the stone cottage was gone, and that a pink glow was coming from the east.

He crashed into a tree before he had gone a dozen steps.

Yesterday there had been no trees within three hundred yards of the cottage.

But that made sense, for there was no cottage any more, and no yesterday. Crush ought to be waiting somewhere out here—except that Crush hadn't got through, and hence didn't really exist.

He went around the tree. It obscured his view of the snake-creature for a moment, and when he tried to find it again, it was gone.

He was glad for the momentary relief, and began looking about him in the half-light. He took a deep breath.

The animals, if they still existed, had vanished with the coming of dawn. The grassy, flower-dotted swards scintillated like emeralds in the early morning haze. From somewhere came the babble of running water.

Meta-universe, by whatever name you called it, was beautiful, like a gorgeous garden. What a pity he must live and die here alone, with nothing but a lot of animals for company. He'd willingly give an arm, or at least a rib, if—

"Adam Prentiss! *Adam!*"

He whirled and stared toward the orchard in elated disbelief.

"E! *Eve!*"

She'd got through!

The whole world, and just the two of them!

His heart was pounding ecstatically as he began to run lithely upwind.

And they'd keep it this way, simple and sweet, forever, and their children after them. To hell with science and progress! (Well, within practical limits, of course.)

As he ran, there rippled about his quivering nostrils the seductive scent of apple blossoms.

THE END